AN UNCERTAIN DEATH

AN
UNCERTAIN DEATH

Jo Bannister

This title first published in Great Britain 1997 by
SEVERN HOUSE PUBLISHERS LTD of
9–15 High Street, Sutton, Surrey SM1 1DF.
Originally published in 1984 under the title
of *Striving With Gods*.
First published in the USA 1997 by
SEVERN HOUSE PUBLISHERS INC., of
595 Madison Avenue, New York, NY 10022.

British Library Cataloguing in Publication Data

Bannister, Jo
         An Uncertain Death
         1. Detective and mystery stories
         1. Title
         823.9'14 [F]

         ISBN 0-7278-5262-0

Printed and bound in Great Britain by
Hartnolls Ltd, Bodmin, Cornwall.

Death closes all: but something ere the end,
Some work of noble note, may yet be done,
Not unbecoming men that strove with Gods.

Ulysses by **Alfred, LordTennyson**

1

ONE

It was long after midnight when the phone rang. I was drowsing over a book. I considered letting it ring, although I was alone and not in bed, because I made a point of not being available round the clock these days. Then I considered picking it up and breathing heavily down it, which my inconsiderate caller would certainly find disconcerting – unless it was my mother, in which case she'd probably breathe heavily back until we both collapsed giggling and hyperventilated. By then I was wide awake, aware that I was being precious, and so I picked the damn thing up.

It wasn't my mother. It was an out-of-town call from a man I didn't know, who introduced himself as a policeman. I asked if he knew what time it was. He asked if I knew Luke Shaw.

'Luke? Yes, of course – why? Oh God, not again.'

Naturally I was concerned, but I'd played this scene before: I didn't take it to heart as much now as I once had. There was, however, no answering levity in the policeman's tone. His voice was quiet and grim, and he sounded tired.

'No. Definitely not again.'

My stomach turned over. The blood raced cold in my veins like melt-water. Luke? Luke had been in and out of scrapes all the years I had known him. There had always been phone calls, always at daft hours, but it was never anything serious. But this was serious. Fingers crawled around my heart and in my hair. I made a wild guess I knew wasn't that wild. 'Is Luke dead?'

There was a pause – the same startled, slightly too long pause you get for asking a doctor to level with you. Then he said in the same slightly, significantly oblique way, 'Are you related to Mr Shaw?'

It wasn't an answer to my question, but it was as good as one. 'No. But I'm the best friend he's got.' That sounded wrong: I rephrased it. 'I was the best friend he had.'

I could hear him breathing. He thought that the longer he put this off the more easily the news would break. I thought about my mother, and part of me wanted to laugh and part of me wanted to cry. Finally the policeman said, 'I'm sorry to have to tell you there's been an accident. Mr Shaw is dead.'

'How?'

'He was carrying your number among his personal effects.' As I carried his, as the person to be contacted first in the event of – an accident?

'How did Luke die?'

He cleared his throat, plainly ill at ease. 'We can't really say yet. There'll be a post-mortem, of course, and an inquest.'

'I want to see him.'

'We would appreciate a formal identification, miss.' The policeman sounded relieved. He'd thought he was going to have to ask me. 'I'll send a car for you.'

'I can drive.'

'Yes, but it's a fair way and you may not be fit to drive back.'

Luke: with his eyes full of sunshine and his blond hair tied in silk knots by the salt wind. Luke on the foredeck of his boat, wrestling with white terylene, laughing at the sky, his round brown face gone all in wrinkles. Gentle Luke, faithful as a spaniel, honest as a martyr. Sweet, sweet Luke. I'd loved him most of my adult life.

Luke dead, on a slab in the morgue, under a sheet that covered all but his poor naked feet, angled at ten to two, a ridiculous label attached to his big toe with a rubber band. Feet are feet, I suppose, if all the toes are present and there are no distinguishing bunions, but I had been on intimate terms with those particular feet for fifteen years. I had shared boats and flats with them. I had given them mustard baths for influenza. I had learnt their look. I knew, before the man in the white coat peeled back the sheet, that no crazy mistake had occurred. No one had taken the wrong jacket from a cloakroom and died carrying Luke's diary. The dead man was my friend.

And dying had hurt and frightened him, and the signs were still plain in his slack, dead face. In a way his face looked less familiar than his feet. Feet don't show suffering, they remain reassuringly the same through most tribulations. Luke's face had changed terribly. Not beyond recognition, but beyond comprehension – mine, at least. Death would account for the utter pallor of his brow, waxen under the neatly combed fringe: they had tidied his hair for my benefit, but they couldn't tidy the fear off his face or rearrange the carven lines of it so that the pain didn't show. I knew those lines. All his character, all his swift and generous emotions, played in them. In life their mobility was delightful, devastating. Now they were softening towards flaccid oblivion, but somewhere in between they had been shocked rigid by what had happened to him in a bed-sitting-room in a boarding house in a Black Country suburb I didn't even know he'd gone to. I remember hoping, without following the implications any further at that stage, that it was not death alone which had done that to him. It was a disquieting thought for the rest of us who had to go the same way.

I must have swayed for I felt someone grip my arms. The man in the white coat covered Luke's white face and the policeman guided me down a corridor to an office and sent for some tea. My hands shook and rattled the cup on the saucer. The sweet warm liquid gagged in my throat.

'How did he die?'

I think I asked several times before I got an answer. I persisted because it seemed necessary to know the reason for the horror in his face; more important, somehow, at that time, than the reason for his body on the slab; as if how he died and why he died were not inextricably linked.

The policeman's name was Marsh. I think I asked him that several times too. He lowered his eyes decently. 'It looks like suicide. His wrists were cut – both of them, up the length of the arteries. It seems he wanted to make a proper job of it.'

'Suicide?' I almost laughed in his face. I put the cup down to save spilling it. 'No. Luke? Never. He wasn't the suicidal type. He was – ' I groped for the right word, found I couldn't do better than the simplest. 'Happy.'

The chief inspector was eyeing me oddly – from under his brows and slightly sideways, and thinking himself the soul of tact. 'Were you very close?'

'I told you. We were as close as two people can be.'

The tact was growing thin, the appraisal more overt. 'Really? I understood – ' Propriety stopped him on the brink.

'He was queer?' I finished for him. 'A queen? A little bit of a wildflower? That's right. Luke was a homosexual. But I told you the truth. As relationships go, love can't hold a candle to real friendship, the kind we had.' I could hear myself talking and it sounded phoney and too loud, but I couldn't stop and anyway it was true. In the fifteen years I knew him we both had lovers, I more than he. But no one was ever closer to Luke than I was, or closer to me than him. That was why the policeman was wrong. 'Anything that happened to Luke that was bad enough to make him want out, I'd know about it. He'd have told me, if only to say goodbye.'

'Perhaps he was afraid you'd try to stop him.'

10

'He was my friend, Mr Marsh. I wouldn't have refused him anything he wanted that badly.'

I saw his policeman's mind chewing that over. If he had suspected a crime he would have been wondering where I might fit into it. He was a big, squarish man, powerfully constructed but no longer in the peak of physical fitness. He was my age or a little older, hovering on the tideline of middle-age, about ready to take the plunge but still putting off the evil moment.

'Miss Rees, a moment ago you told me Luke Shaw wasn't the suicidal type. Now you seem to be saying he'd do it if the circumstances were right. Which is it?'

It was both, of course, and he should have known at least as well as me that given the right reasons we are all capable of suicide, just as we are all capable of murder. Luke might have killed himself to avoid the dreary, distasteful closing act of a terminal illness, or if his life had become a burden to someone he cared about. But he would have thought it through – I still believed he would have talked to me about it – and then he would have done it calmly, maybe a little sadly, but confident in his right to choose and the wisdom of that choice. He would not have died with his fallen-angel face screwed up in shock and terror. His death had been done to him.

As my mind gradually came to terms with it, I became quite certain that Luke had been murdered, and in a way it made it easier. The last minutes of his life had been frightful. I pictured him struggling with his enemies – hopelessly, he wasn't the martial type – the blond hair flying, terror in his eyes and no one to help him. But better that, I thought, than the months of bleak despair it would have taken to reduce him to suicide. I felt the sense of slight within me wane, and the anger begin to wax.

'You said, a post-mortem?'

Marsh nodded. 'It's a formality, of course.'

11

'Formality my eye. You're going to need what it can tell you. Luke was murdered.'

I suppose policemen are used to extraordinary statements from the bereaved. Certainly he didn't leap up and start hunting his pockets for his magnifying glass and deerstalker. He said politely, 'Can you explain that?'

I couldn't, not very well. I tried, but it quickly became obvious that I wasn't getting through. Even to myself I didn't sound to be making too much sense. But it was as I had said – it came down to a question of happiness. With less reason than most, Luke had always been a supremely happy man: a born optimist with a gift for contentment. If something had happened to destroy that happiness, I'd have known. I believed absolutely that he'd have told me. Therefore it wasn't suicide.

'It's perfectly possible to slash someone else's wrists, you know,' I finished tartly.

'Perfectly,' he agreed. 'But most people would not lie obligingly still on their beds for the length of time it takes to bleed to death.' My knees went weak again at the thought of pint after pint of Luke's blood coursing down over the covers and pooling on the floor. Marsh didn't notice, or at least didn't stop. 'If there'd been any kind of a struggle we'd have found blood all over the room. And – '

Finally he stopped. He had a fine sense of delicacy, this policeman, who was reduced to blushes by the word homosexual but was perfectly happy to describe in graphic detail my friend's recent gory demise. Anger at him stiffened my nerve. 'And? There's more?'

He looked unhappy. We were back on his idea of sensitive ground. 'I'm afraid so. There was a boy with him, also dead. It looks very much like – ' he shrugged and grimaced – 'a suicide pact.'

I'd thought those went out with Fortuny dresses and sipping champagne from slippers, but the other thing I was

12

thinking was more important. 'A boy?' It wasn't so much an exclamation as an exultation and it must have carried through half the building, turning the heads that rigor mortis had not yet immobilised. Incredibly, I felt myself beginning to grin. 'No.'

Marsh was finding my maverick reactions as unsettling as the notion of a happy homosexual. 'I assure you, Miss Rees—'

'Oh, I don't doubt you, Mr Marsh. It confirms every instinct I had about this. Luke was murdered, and it was made to look like suicide, only they made a bad mistake when they used a boy. Luke never went with boys.'

He was frowning, but at least he was listening. 'Can you be sure of that?'

'Absolutely sure.' Certainty, a crazy kind of gladness and a crazier kind of pride swelled in me. I trembled with the sense of conquest. An abstract, esoteric conquest it was, like climbing a mountain that looms no less high afterwards than before; the situation was not changed, but my perspective was. Marsh could as easily disregard my views on this as on previous points, but before I was relying on instinct, on faith. Now I knew. 'For two reasons. Luke always said he was twenty-two before he knew for sure where his sexuality lay, he would have no part in confusing children who didn't know what they were or what they wanted. But if you don't accept that, go down the hall and look at him again. He was beautiful, Mr Marsh. He was small and blond, he'd a smile like a shy angel's and eyes you could dance to. He was never the senior partner in his life.'

I was embarrassing the poor man again. 'You mean—'

I took a malicious pleasure in spelling it out. 'I mean, he was more sinned upon than sinning. His lovers were always older men. He was thirty-two – sometimes he looked twenty. He was a sodomite's dream.'

The policeman looked doubtful. 'He doesn't look twenty to me.'

13

I met his eyes. 'You're not seeing him at his best, though, are you?'

I didn't know the boy. I hadn't expected to, and I thought it unlikely that Luke had either. They were from different worlds. Everything about the skimpy, wasted body marked him as a derelict. He couldn't have been more than sixteen, but his face was hollowed by the rigours of living rough. There were half-healed sores on his neck that looked as if they could still have been there if he'd lived twice as long. His hair was long and ragged, his skin unhealthy – well, it would be, wouldn't it, but it must have been for a long time before he died – and everything about his pathetic little corpse was ill-kempt. His toenails wert overgrown and some of them were broken. A year or eighteen months ago he had been someone's son: a trial, no doubt, difficult and sullen as teenage boys are, but loved by someone. At the time of his death he was as near nothing as a human being can get.

But if he had died in the same place as Luke and at the same time, he had not died the same way. There was no fear in his face, no pain, only a kind of slack-mouthed pleasure, an improbable smile. 'I take it you've looked for needle marks.'

Marsh shot me another curious, sidelong look. 'Yes, he was a user. Had been for a while, and from the state of his arms not too particular where he got the needles. Miss Rees, how do you happen to know so much about this kind of thing?'

'Doctor Rees.'

'Oh. Oh!' He did a double-take, lingering the second time to absorb the size 10 jeans, the T-shirt, the sneakers and the windcheater, then expanding his view to take in my face. Until that moment I honestly don't think he knew I was a woman pushing forty. He was going over everything I'd said, that he'd taken with a pinch of salt, in the light of my new-found authority. 'So – Mr Shaw was your patient?'

14

'Don't be bloody silly. I keep telling you: we were close, close friends. I cared about him – not the broad, intellectual caring you want from your doctor but a pointed, personal kind that meant I could no more treat him than I could my mother. Listen. I knew Luke for fifteen years. We shared flats. Sometimes we split up to share with other people, but when the other people got boring or demanding or found other people of their own, we always ended up together again. I loved him, Mr Marsh, every way that matters. I want to know why he died, and why he died in a rooming house in a grotty little Midlands town where so far as I know he had no friends and no interests. I want to know who killed him, and I want to see those people hurting like I'm hurting now. And the first step towards all of that is a thorough post-mortem, so that we know exactly how he died. The bastards who did it went to a lot of trouble to keep that from us, so it would be no bad thing to find out, would it? Don't you think?'

Chief Inspector Marsh eyed me with the dazed expression of a man savaged by a hamster. He was still thinking that women doctors of mature years ought to wear bras under their T-shirts, even when there was nothing in there worth propping up.

TWO

There was lint in his lungs, from a big Berber cushion that was part of the furnishings in his furnished room. The rooming house called itself a residential hotel and filled its apartments with colonial souvenirs that someone clearly thought raised the tone of the place towards the genteel. Luke, who was gentle but never genteel, had taken a bedsitter for a month and on the third night someone had used the big Berber cushion to smother him.

Not to death: nothing so crude, so obvious. They had used it to crush the fight out of him because fists would have left bruises. They had allowed him just enough air to keep him alive, so that his heart could pump the blood out of his slit wrists. His face was twisted up the way it was because his last conscious memories were the sharp pain in his arms, the deep burning pain of his starved lungs, and the sure expectation of death.

Chief Inspector Marsh drove down to London to tell me officially that it was now a murder enquiry. He found me packing my bags. His surprise at that was as nothing beside his total stupefaction when I told him where I was going.

'Luke Shaw's room? You're moving into Luke Shaw's room in Skipley? You're moving into the room where Luke Shaw was murdered?'

'They're having the carpet steam-cleaned and the bedding bleached.'

16

He stared at me, his broad face gone still, a sharpness in his eyes compounded of a little respect and more disgust. 'You are one cool lady,' he said quietly.

I raised my head to look straight at him. 'I want to know what he was doing there. Why he was in bloody Skipley at all, and why he expected to stay a month. What was the boy doing in the room, and who was he? I want to know what happened.'

'They're good questions, but finding the answers is my job,' Marsh said stiffly.

'So is separating the suicides from the murders.' He flushed darkly. I knew I was being unfair, but I was feeling rough enough without having to justify myself to him. I didn't apologise but I did try to explain. 'Chief Inspector, do you believe in ghosts?'

He had thought his capacity for astonishment exhausted. He had been wrong. His eyebrows climbed like racing Sherpas and disappeared into his hairline. 'Ghosts? Good God, no. Do you?'

'I have an open mind. I don't find the idea of an existence after death inconceivable: God knows, what comes before isn't much cop. All I'm saying is that if there are ghosts Luke is probably now qualified, and if he comes back to haunt the scene of his demise I want to be there.'

Marsh squinted at me suspiciously. He was right, I was pulling his leg, but not altogether. I didn't expect to see something white and wafty wearing my friend's shy angel smile in the crook of its left arm flitting round the house without using the doors. But on those days with an R in them, when I entertain the possibility of the paranormal, it seems to me that one of the options is that places, maybe objects too, may carry an imprint of the events they witness, like a tape recording sounds, and that the quality of such impressions might intensify in direct proportion to the emotional content involved, so that the most potent images

17

might somehow impinge on the audio-visual frequencies. On Thursdays, Fridays and Saturdays, in short, I considered it just possible that Luke's furniture might tip me the wink as to what happened to him. Even on Sundays through Wednesdays I thought that living for a few days in the place where he died might give me some clue as to what took him there.

Marsh wouldn't have believed me even if I'd managed to explain all that. I knew full well that when he left he would look into the possibility of my standing to gain by Luke's death. I didn't care. There was nothing to find. Luke might have bequeathed me a few personal treasures, but he never hung on to money for long and anyway a blind man could have seen that no nest egg for my old age would soften the loss I had suffered. In the middle of me there was an aching void where Luke used to be, and the only thing I could think of that would help dull the pain was vengeance. Call it justice if it makes you feel happier, dealing with Luke's murderer would serve both ends, but then and for some time afterwards my thinking was strictly along Old Testament lines. It was not the due process of law I craved so much as blood.

I had thought I was over the shock, but it hit me afresh, with the force of a blow, when I shut the door on Luke's fusty little flat and stood alone in the place where he had choked and bled his life away. I felt the tears prickle and then surge; grief and rage dragged my mouth an ugly shape, and I dropped my bags and stood among them crying my heart out, not covering my face because there was both honour and dignity in mourning for Luke. There was even a little comfort.

When I was done crying I sat on the bed and looked round. Insofar as he decently could the landlord had left it as Luke had found it a week before because that was what I had asked for. I sat and looked round and wondered what had been important enough to make my sybaritic friend sentence himself to a month in these surroundings. There was nothing wrong with either the room or the house, particularly if you feel drawn to red plush, brass gongs and elephant-foot umbrella stands. But Luke's was an exquisite sensitivity. He cherished the delicate and the fine. His spiritual home was the Japanese garden, not the hill stations of the British Raj. This musty, dusty room with its atmosphere of memsahibs, ayahs and tiffin would have been painfully uncongenial for him. Yet he had come here, had planned to spend a month and in fact spent the rest of his life among these souvenirs of empire. In God's name, why?

As I had been disturbed in packing by Chief Inspector Marsh, so I was discovered unpacking by Ben Sawyer. The doorbell buzzed – a harsh, peremptory sound that would never have been permitted to ruffle the tranquility of a British Indian afternoon – and I answered it with an arm full of clothes, wondering what I should say if it was someone looking for Luke.

It was a tall, pleasant-looking man in his mid thirties, slightly academic in appearance, unfashionably well-groomed right down to his highly polished shoes. People my height notice shoes. Above the sombre smile of his brown eyes, his brown hair was neatly cut; his long capable hands, scrubbed and ringless, were folded in front of him.

'Dr Rees?'

'Yes?'

'I'm Ben Sawyer, from the hospital. Chief Inspector Marsh said I'd find you here.'

His voice was quiet, beautifully modulated, just touched with an acceptable amount of respect. I looked at his deft, scrubbed hands. 'You're the pathologist.'

'I wanted to thank you,' he said. 'Every pathologist dreads missing something like that. Thanks to you, I knew what to look for.'

He didn't look the careless sort. 'You'd have found it. I expect you've seen more suicides than I have. They don't

19

look how Luke looked.'

He shrugged self-deprecatingly. 'It's always possible to miss the obvious – to concentrate on the scientific and neglect the human. Anyway, I just wanted to say thanks – and, I'm sorry about your friend.' He hovered on the threshold, unwilling to intrude. He would have left if I'd wanted him to.

I opened the door wider. 'Come in. I'll make some coffee.'

He made the coffee, in Luke's tiny kitchen. By the time I'd found places to hang my clothes he had found the cups and the coffee, and a bottle of five-day-old milk in the fridge. When it wouldn't pour, even when held upside down and slapped like a new baby, we threw it out and did without.

'Harry Marsh said you were very close, you and – Luke.'

I raised an eyebrow. 'You know our chief inspector then?'

'Occupational hazard,' he said with a quick grin, 'getting friendly with policemen. If you seek treatment it's tax deductable.'

I smiled back and decided to answer his question. 'Yes, Luke and I have been friends a long time.'

'The news must have been shattering.'

'It was.'

'Harry Marsh said – ' He stopped abruptly and blushed.

'That I'm a cold-blooded cow?'

Ben Sawyer nodded slowly. 'Something like that. He's wrong, though, isn't he?'

I returned his smile and felt the warmth of his understanding seep into my bones, which had lain chill since the night the phone rang. 'Yes, he's wrong.'

We talked, of course, about medicine. I told him that I hadn't practiced for three years, that I'd been writing instead. It wasn't the most regular of incomes but the lifestyle was a lot pleasanter. My mother thought me mad but my ulcer approved.

Ben looked suitably impressed. 'What do you write – articles, books?'

'Books. Five in the last six years, that got published. An almost infinite number in the years before which didn't, and quite right too.'

'Medical textbooks?'

'Murder mysteries.'

I said it as deadpan as I could, expressionless of face and voice, and he didn't know if I was joking or absolutely serious. I was absolutely serious, but in the circumstances of course it was pretty funny. Ben floundered and I offered no help. His conversations with Chief Inspector Marsh had not prepared him for this because, for fairly obvious reasons, Chief Inspector Marsh had not been told. It didn't matter if he knew now, but if he had known that first night Luke's file would have been stamped Suicide and closed. The MB had served me well.

Finally Ben said, 'They really knew what they were doing when they picked on your friend, didn't they?' We smiled at each other and things became easier again.

He asked how we'd met, Luke and I, and since it was a good story I told him. 'He got a puncture and I stopped to change his wheel.'

Ben laughed. 'Now you *are* having me on.'

'No, but it wasn't quite how it sounds either. He was trying to do it one-handed. Someone had stamped on his other hand a few days before and broken three fingers.'

I'd learnt to judge people by their reactions to this charming little anecdote. Quite a number just shrug and nod, as if it was about what they'd expect and I was naive for expecting different.

Ben Sawyer looked shocked and faintly sick. 'Good God. Why? Because –?'

'Yes. Some fine upstanding example of British manhood objected to sharing the street with a queer.' I heard the bitterness in my own voice. It had happened half a dozen times in the fifteen years I knew him, but I never got over the sense of outrage, the quaking anger I felt at the injustice of it. 'Ben, you should have known him – there wasn't a more inoffensive soul alive. I know homosexuals can be a pain but not Luke, it wasn't his style. He was quiet. I don't know how anyone knew just by looking at him, except that he was gentle and quiet at a time when most young men were making a virtue out of violence.'

And at a time when I was still thinking it would be nice if it turned out he was normal after all, I wondered why he wouldn't make the small effort necessary to pass as hetero-sexual. He was never promiscuous, didn't need sex as some do – men and women – for the constant reassurance. He went happily celibate for months or years at a time when there was no one special around. But when there was he found the same deep emotional and physical satisfaction as everyone else in expanding affection to include the ultimate, intimate sharing of bodies. And the reason he would not cross the line between discretion and deceit was that he saw nothing wrong in a way of life that suited him and hurt no one, and he was too honest and too stubborn to pretend to be something he was not. So every couple of years I'd find him in plaster and tears, having been beaten into the ground by some animal twice his size who wouldn't begin to understand about love if he lived to be ninety.

About that point in the conversation I became aware that we had both slipped down from our chairs to squat among cushions on the red mock-Turkey carpet, intermittently rest-ing cups and elbows on the beaten brass coffee-table, as if it was the most natural thing in the world and anyway we had known each other for years. There was nothing heady or portentious in our familiarity; it was an easy thing, born of common interests and a perhaps childish lack of concern with our own images. I felt Luke's presence in the amiable ethos like a benign maitre d' supervising a favourite corner table. I thought he would have approved of Ben.

But I was also aware that if he was still there ten minutes later, soothing my soul with his calm brown eyes and the quiet length of him sprawled on my carpet, I should want him to stay. I would ask him to stay and he would stay, and though there would be comfort in the night, the days and all the successive days would be guilty with the spectre of exploitation. My emotions were still too tattered to admit anyone new without knotting and tangling irresolvably about him, and I wanted better than that for both of us. So I got up and found his jacket and smiled, and he smiled and put it on and left. I knew without asking that he would be back. He knew without asking that he would be welcome.

I slept like a log in Luke's bed.

THREE

In the morning, starting over breakfast, I tried to take stock of what I was doing and why. I had conceived my plan while still in a state of shock and put it into effect while the novelty, and a racy bravado I had mistaken for courage and which in retrospect I found rather distasteful, were running high. In the cold clear light of day, now the shock was dissipating and the novelty tarnished and my mood of emotional flagellation discovered for the self-indulgence it was, I faced up to the questions of what had brought me here, whether I should stay, and if so what I hoped to achieve.

The best reason for being in his flat was not that Luke had died here but that for a short time he had lived here. There was a kind of healing in the place where he had spent his last days: it was the closest I could get to him now. And that was about all I could find on the credit side. Remove that and all which remained was a morbid middle-aged woman wallowing in her grief in a bizarre fashion because there were no normal ways of expressing that particular bereavement. If I had lost my husband or lover, or my brother or son, or even a professional colleague, a sympathetic world would have hastened to offer its condolences; and if its compassion would have done nothing to soften the loss it might at least have diluted the loneliness. But the world had never understood my love for Luke. It found our necessarily platonic relationship disturbing, unnatural. My other friends had fought shy

24

of Luke in life and now he was dead could not express genuine regret. Implicit in their voices and at the back of their eyes was the opinion that I was better off without him. But I didn't feel better. I felt sick, bereft, incomplete – as if someone had stolen not my friend but my arm or eyes. Without Luke I felt like an amputee, a cripple.

Ben Sawyer, I recognised this morning, had served the need that should have been met by those delicate, dilatory friends. He had listened and not judged. And that was why, this morning and not before, I could see the pathetic absurdity of my gesture. It had seemed gravely odd to Harry Marsh. Now it looked pretty odd to me too. I smiled to myself, ruefully, feeling my sense of proportion wobble to its feet and take a few tottery steps. I thought I would wait until Ben came round and ask him to help me pack again.

With a mug of coffee in one hand, a slice of toast in the other and no plate – marking my progress therefore by a trail of crumbs which, had he been there, Luke would have been vacuuming up almost before they hit the carpet, like an indignant bloodhound in hot pursuit of an escaped convict – I wandered round the room, finding a certain dry amusement in the absolute absurdity of my surroundings. It was then that I saw the books.

I was still puzzling over them when Ben arrived, shortly after ten. He had not said he was coming. I didn't even know what hours he worked. But it didn't occur to me that the knock at the door could be anyone else, and we greeted each other as casually as if he'd just nipped out to feed the parking meter.

'Ben, was there anything wrong with his kidneys?'

He looked surprised and bent over to see what I was reading. 'Luke's? Wrong in what way?'

'Disease, dysfunction – any way. Anything that would have made him go out and buy two books on renal failure and dialysis.' I showed him. 'These didn't come with the rent book.'

'There was nothing wrong with his kidneys. He was as fit as a dead man can be.' It was the sort of joke doctors make daily among themselves. Remembering my interest was not professional he winced. 'Sorry.'

I grinned, almost without trying. 'It's all right, I'm past the maudlin stage. But I don't understand these.' They were big, expensive, devastatingly detailed volumes written not even so much for doctors as for medical scientists. I wouldn't have bought them, and I couldn't imagine why Luke had. Especially since, if he'd wanted to read about kidneys, he had only to ask for my copy of Barnes. I suggested as much to Ben. 'Surely he's still the authority on renal failure?'

'Barnes?'

'Julian Barnes. There can't be a medical library in the country without his *Causes & Treatments* on the shelf. Jesus, Ben, you're not going to tell me he's before your time?'

'Of course not,' he said hastily. 'He'd be my first choice. But I'm a doctor, Clio, like you. Maybe Luke didn't know about Barnes.'

'He knew, all right. He'd met Barnes – I introduced them in a bar in London, not six months ago. Julian promised to send me a copy of the new edition. If he was so interested, why didn't Luke ask me for it?'

'Perhaps he forgot the conversation. You say Barnes is your friend rather than Luke's?'

'Yes,' I agreed doubtfully. 'Well, friend is probably stretching a point; these days at least. I saw a bit of him when we were younger. But Luke wouldn't forget. He had extra-ordinary memory – it might have been something to do with his job.'

'What was his job, exactly?'

'Microprocessors.'

He blinked. People always blinked at the thought of Luke Shaw as an electronics wizard. A hairdresser, perhaps, or a

26

dancer, or even an art critic – but electronics? But he had a very orderly mind coupled with a kind of synaptic deftness, and I believe from those who were qualified to know that he was good enough to be disconcerting.

'He worked at ComIntel, in London. Systems design. I wonder if they've been told.'

'I expect Harry Marsh called them.' He spoke absently, as if at least part of his mind was elsewhere. I remembered that I didn't actually know why he was here.

'Ben, was there something you wanted to tell me?'

He gave me a hunted look that hit me under the heart and knocked the wind out. I didn't know what was coming, only that I wasn't going to like it. 'I meant to tell you yesterday. Better you hear it from me than from Harry Marsh or at the inquest.'

I stood frozen, stiff as an icicle and probably as white, waiting. 'What is it, Ben?' My voice surprised both of us by coming out quite calm.

He cast around the room uneasily. 'Shouldn't you sit down?' He had absolutely no bedside manner: from having only dead patients, I suppose.

'What is it?' I felt the warmth and tension gather behind my knees, where the shaking would start.

'Luke,' he said, unnecessarily. It was a measure of his discomfiture. 'I found something else, something that maybe – changes the complexion of the thing. There were no bruises on him, he hadn't been beaten, but there were the beginnings of a bruise in the middle of his chest. He had been hit – perhaps once, more like a number of times in the same place – hard blows, directly to the sternum.'

I thought about it and my eyes began to burn. He was describing an attempt to restart a failed heart. 'Someone tried to save him?'

'I can't think what else it would mean.'

But I could. That's the trouble with thinking: once you

27

start you can't stop just because you've got where you want to be. If your answer doesn't sit right with the facts, usually it isn't right, and much as I would have liked to believe that when Luke was dying there was someone there who cared enough to try and stop it, logically it wouldn't work. As a writer I wouldn't have scripted it that way, and neither would chance. Sounding like Cassandra even in my own ears, I told Ben why.

'Consider the situation. These bastards are bleeding Luke to make his death look like suicide. Then someone comes along who tries to save him. What happens then? If he chased off the bastards and gave Luke cardiac massage, it might have worked or it might not but even if it didn't, why would he disappear right afterwards without reporting the murder?

'Or perhaps it did work. Were the bruises you found sufficiently formed to suggest that he lived for at least a short time afterwards?' Ben inclined his head in sombre acknowledgment. 'So why didn't he whistle up an ambulance and do the job properly? If somebody wanted to save Luke's life, and in fact got his heart beating again, why did he die? And why did no one know until a neighbour got ratty over the loud music?'

Ben's open face was creased up, perplexed. 'Then – what do you suppose happened?'

I clasped my arms about me as if the room had turned suddenly cold. 'These are bastards we're dealing with, right? So we'd better figure on them behaving like bastards. I don't think there was an angel of mercy dashing to the rescue, too late or at all. I think they made it too difficult for him to breathe and his heart packed up before it had pumped out enough blood for their scenario to be convincing. If they wanted a suicide verdict they had to keep his heart going long enough for him to bleed to death. And they did, and he did.'

I closed my eyes. Projected inside the lids I saw it happen:

the small blond figure sprawled limply on the bed, blood on the covers but not enough, not yet, the big Berber cushion cast aside. They had his shirt open and one of them beat his fist down with measured force on the breastbone, and maybe bent over the white face to lay his mouth on the blue lips in a monstrous parody of a kiss. And when the starved lungs responded and the starved blood began to spurt, they picked up the cushion again and kept him hovering on the brink of consciousness until death supervened. I suppose men have been killed in more cold-blooded ways, but not too many of them. My knees didn't shake. They gave out altogether. I dropped like a stone.

Ben caught me awkwardly, steering me into a chair, his face stunned and ghostly pale. He stammered, 'This is pure speculation – '

And of course it was, but not to me. To me it was revelation. I *knew* what had happened to Luke. I also knew something else, something which had been kicking around in the back of my brain for some time and only needed this last burst of mental activity to crystalise into understanding. 'Jesus, Ben, you know what we're talking about, don't you?' My voice came reedy and breathless, laced with horror and with awe. 'We're saying the man who did this was one of us. Luke was murdered by a doctor.'

Ben straightened up with a jerk, shocked to the core. I might have accused him of practising necrophilia. His eyes were round and hurt. If he had believed it he would have been appalled but all his instincts, all his training and experience, fought against belief. 'Clio, that's absurd!'

'No, it's not. Think about it.'

'Even if we're right about the bruising, you don't need to be a doctor to learn resuscitation techniques these days. They teach it in first-aid classes, swimming pools – '

'Yes, mouth-to-mouth. They also print easy-to-follow diagrams in women's magazines. But cardiac massage is in a different league, Ben. That's a game for experts – people like you and me. And this bastard, whoever he is.

'Consider what we know about him. He knows how to commit a murder that looks like suicide except under the most detailed examination. He knows that for a really efficient haemorrhage you cut the arteries lengthwise – ninety-nine people out of a hundred would cut them across. I bet there were no hesitation marks.' I raised my eyebrows at him and Ben shook his head silently. I nodded. 'Also, he can judge suffocation so finely that he can use a cushion as a valve, letting in just enough air to keep Luke alive and not so much that he starts getting lively. And when Luke's heart stops beating he knows it's too soon and he knows what to do about it. He's a doctor, all right. Jesus Christ, Ben, there's a doctor out there going round murdering people.'

There was a long, long pause. Then he said, 'People?'

I don't think I have a particularly quick brain, only that some folk have particularly slow ones. 'The boy, Ben. You don't think his OD was a coincidence?'

He sat down heavily. 'I'd forgotten him,' he admitted. 'Look, Clio, I think we're getting awfully deep into this. We're not detectives – this isn't our world. With your help, I've given the police all the information those two bodies were capable of yielding, at least to me. Can't we leave the deductions to those who have the knowledge and experience to make them?'

'If I'd left it to the police they'd have written Luke off as a suicide,' I reminded him coldly. 'How did the boy die?'

'Heroin.'

'And you can't say before Luke or after?'

'Probably afterwards. It would have taken a little time.'

So maybe they fixed him up first, poor nameless sod, and let him sit there, grinning his idiot grin as he slid into a happy stupor, while they used the same ruthless efficiency and specialist knowledge to murder Luke. The other man's terrified struggles would have meant nothing to him. His veiled eyes, the pupils shrunk to pin-points under the drooping lids, would have seen the frantic, doomed efforts of a man hardly stronger than himself to escape from people who had come prepared for their task and would have seen him quickly subdued; his ears would have heard the cries and later the muffled coughing of famished lungs begging for air. He would have watched Luke bleeding and choking, and if he thought anything it was probably just that TV these days was all sex and violence and wasn't it fun? I pictured him slumped against the wall, intermittently giggling to himself, unaware that he too was dying. In all likelihood he never knew.

'The noise,' I said suddenly to Ben. 'There must have been some noise – at first, when he was jumped. They couldn't have kept him quiet without marking him, not until they got the cushion over his face. Why did nobody hear him? These are goddamn bed-sitters, why did nobody hear him scream?'

The man on one side was elderly and half deaf. The woman of a middle-aged couple answered the door on the other side. I introduced myself briefly. 'The night Luke Shaw was murdered. Didn't you hear anything?'

She resented being asked, inferring some criticism in my question. She had already told the police, she said. The radio was on very loud all evening in Luke's flat: that was all she heard. When it was still on at midnight she complained to the landlord. He, getting no reply to door or telephone, used his key, and the police were on the scene ten minutes later.

It made sense. I thanked her and, dispirited, turned away. She stopped me with a tentative hand. 'I may have heard something else. I'm not sure. At nine o'clock there was a short break on the radio, between the end of the programme and the start of the news. I thought I heard – ' She trailed off, uncertain, twisting a handkerchief between her fingers.

'What? Please, it could be important.'

31

'A whimper,' she said then. 'As if he had a dog in there. A little whimper like a frightened dog.'

FOUR

Ben Sawyer came with me to see Chief Inspector Marsh, for which I was grateful. I was grateful when we went in and even more grateful when we came out.

I told him about the woman next door. I told him about the radio and how she had complained to the landlord, and he listened with mounting impatience and finally interrupted. 'Yes, Dr Rees, we did actually know all that. It did actually occur to us to speak to the neighbours.'

I told him about the break before the news and the sound like a frightened dog. 'Did you actually know that Luke was in the process of being murdered at nine o'clock precisely?'

He hadn't. He consulted the papers on his desk. 'That would appear to fit in with the estimated time of death.'

'Estimated times of death are just that,' I informed him tartly, 'estimates. There are too many variables for accuracy. I'm giving you an exact time. The people who killed Luke entered that house before nine pm and left after nine. Someone must have seen them.'

Veins were beginning to stand proud at the policeman's temples. Another ten years and he could have a real problem with blood pressure. And do you know what that's bad for? – kidneys.

'The front door,' he said stiffly, 'is left on the latch until ten. Before that anyone can come in. Even after that anyone can let himself out and slam the door behind him. It was

Friday night: half the residents were going out, the other half were having friends in. The front hall must have been like Snowhill Station. Nobody saw anything suspicious, and I'd have been very surprised if they had done.'

'Nothing suspicious?' My voice rose shrilly. 'It took a minimum of three men to kill Luke, and they brought a sixteen-year-old heroin addict in with them. You consider that normal Friday night traffic in a Skipley rooming house?'

'Don't shout at me, Dr Rees!'

We glared at one another, silently pugnacious, from a range of inches. Ben interceded, tactfully letting some of the heat out. 'Have you identified the boy yet, Harry?'

Marsh dragged his eyes away from me. 'No, not yet. We're working on it. You'd be amazed how many teenage boys disappear off the face of the earth each year. You would,' he added pointedly, glaring at me once more. 'She wouldn't. I bet you she knows already.' He paused and his tone dropped a note as he back-tracked. 'Why do you say it took three men to kill him? He didn't look particularly strong.'

'He wasn't strong at all. A determined ten-year-old could have overpowered him. It wasn't Luke but the way they chose to kill him that took the manpower. Because they wanted it to look like suicide they had to kill him slowly, and they also had to do it without knocking him about. That takes strong hands and several of them: as an absolute minimum, one man holding the cushion to his face and one on each arm so he didn't spray blood around the place with struggling. Try holding someone quite still and you'll see what I mean. Think of a child in a tantrum: unless you're prepared to hurt it you can't keep it still. Then think of a man fighting for his life.'

I told him about my doctor theory. He didn't seem particularly impressed. I told him about the books, and specifically about the book that wasn't there, and he looked downright sceptical. Truth to tell, it was beginning to sound a bit flimsy to me too. You don't always get the ideal, in any of life's regards. Sometimes you settle for second best, either in ignorance or because it's easier, more convenient, cheaper, or still plenty good enough for your needs. Luke might have opted for less highly regarded books rather than wait if the Barnes was out of stock; and he might have preferred not to ask for mine for the same reason he didn't tell me he was coming to Skipley for a month.

That still rankled. I didn't understand why he had come here, I didn't understand why he had died here – in surroundings he could never have chosen and in company I didn't believe he had sought – but most of all I didn't understand why he hadn't told me. He told me if he was going to the dentist: what was so specially secret about Skipley?

I was thinking of telling the chief inspector that I was thinking of going home when he asked if I was thinking of going home yet. I bristled. 'Certainly not.'

He breathed heavily. 'Dr Rees, I can't see what it is you hope to achieve here. You've been very helpful, by virtue both of your professional skill and your personal knowledge. But the work to be done now is all police work, and I don't see how you can help with that.'

My bristles grew bristles. 'This may come as a cruel surprise to you, Chief Inspector, but when people are organising their lives there are other considerations beside what is helpful to you.'

'And when other people's lives are being cut forcibly short, he snarled, 'it is my duty to find those responsible, everybody else's duty to render such assistance as they can, and the duty of those who can't to keep the bloody hell out of my way!'

I don't know what colour I was. He was a fetching shade of purple.

Ben said sharply, 'Harry!' He wasn't used to hearing women spoken to like that. On the other hand, he wasn't used to his visitors giving him a hard time either. Pathology's not a bad line if you prefer clients who don't answer back.

Marsh stopped snarling. He raked his fingers through his hair once, took several deep breaths, had a short circular prowl round his office and came back to the desk. He looked at me as if I had been specially run up by hell to torment him. 'All right,' he said, 'fine. You want to wallow in it, go right ahead and wallow. I can't kick you out of town and I've no grounds for locking you up. But I will advise you that it may not be only my nose you're getting up.

'Somebody thought he'd committed an undetectable murder. Now he knows he didn't, he probably knows you're the reason he didn't, and if he thinks you're likely to balls up his activities any further he may want you out of the way more than I do, only he won't draw the line at shouting. Loath as I am to suggest this, Dr Rees, but if you insist on staying in Skipley, then for your own safety I think you ought to keep in touch with the station here.'

I was taken aback by his words, which struck me sober like cold water in the face. I had not thought of that. He was right, of course, and it was good of him to be concerned. Unfortunately, I lack the gift of graceful gratitude. 'Would you like me to report daily,' I asked snidely, 'and should I stay clear of bars and pool halls?'

'Suit yourself,' he said coldly, showing us out.

I drove Ben to his hospital before heading for home – my present home, that is to say, carpets, gongs and all. People hadn't stopped dying because we knew how Luke had died. It was a fairly typical suburban hospital: built in the '30s, extended in the '60s, short of money in the '80s. Now the original red-brick buildings were interspersed with prefabricated structures and the place looked a little like a polytechnic and a little like a refugee camp.

As Ben got out I said, 'You don't suppose he's serious, do you – about these bastards coming after me?'

He smiled – at the rueful compound of bravado, alarm and

selfconscious embarrassment in my voice, I supposed. It was a warm and friendly smile, touched at the edges by a not unsympathetic amusement. 'With machine-guns in violin cases, you mean? I don't think so. Oh, I agree with Harry, I think you'd be better off back in London, but not because anybody's going to make you a cement swimsuit otherwise. I just don't think you're doing any good here – not for Luke, not for yourself.'

I forced a grin. 'You don't think I'm so close to cracking it I should invest in a Doberman?'

Ben's smile faded. His brows drew together in a frown. 'Is that what you're trying to do – crack it? Is that why you're staying on?'

'Harry Marsh thinks I'm wallowing.'

'I'd sooner think you were wallowing than that you were taking on the people who murdered Luke. Clio, you're not qualified, you're not equipped – '

'I'm not taking them on, Ben. I don't know who they are.'

'Then what are you doing?'

'When I work that out, you'll be the first to know.' I drove on, leaving him standing there.

That afternoon I got a new neighbour. The basement room directly below mine had been empty since I arrived. The sounds of someone taking possession – cupboards being investigated, drawers explored, the rattle of wire hangers in the wardrobe – rose slightly muffled through the floor and the mock-Turkey carpet.

I was engaged in a curious exercise. I had a sheet of paper in my typewriter – I could no more have left it in London than leave my hot-water bottle behind – and I was setting out the known elements of Luke's death as I set out notes for a novel. I thought, I think, that seeing them in that familiar format might help me to consider them objectively and constructively. It didn't, not to any noticeable degree, but still I was reluctant to break off and investigate the activities below. I had not been there long enough, nor did I intend staying long enough, to warrant curiosity about a new tenant. I went on staring at my notes until the lamp over my makeshift desk went out. I tried the main light switch and that too was dead. Brusque with fatigue and frustration, I stalked out into the dim hall and growled down the basement stairs, 'What the hell is going on down there?'

A yellow head appeared in the gloomy stairwell. 'Hello. Do you know where the fusebox is?'

'Fusebox?'

'My wiring looks it was cannibalised off the Ark. One socket sparks, another's dead and I think the cooker just blew the whole house.'

'Where's the landlord?'

'That's what I'd like to know. He must have heard me filling the kettle. He's probably hurrying down to the claims office with his fire insurance in his hot little hand.'

Mr Pinner was a great many things but a cowboy wasn't one. He made respectability a vice. I giggled at the prospect of him as an arsonist. Footsteps sounded on the stair.

The yellow head belonged to a young man in his middle twenties with a longish goat-thin face, seagreen eyes, and a pair of jeans that should have been given to a scarecrow long enough since and indeed might well have been. His sweat-shirt insisted 'Whales are beautiful' but disproved its claim by showing a picture of one. The seagreen eyes looked at me severely. He was of average height but the string-thinness of him made him seem tall. He might have been a male model for Oxfam.

He said sternly, 'The situation is anything but risible,' which of course turned it from mildly humorous to utterly hilarious and had us clinging to the stair-rail and one another for support before Mr Pinner returned and fixed the fuse, one alarmed eye all the while keeping watch over his shoulder in case we got too close.

Charlie – that was his name, Charlie Brown, but he didn't have a beagle, I asked – invited me down for a flat-warming. But as well as not having a beagle he hadn't any milk and he couldn't find any cups, so we ended up warming his flat from the comparative comfort of mine. While I made coffee he inspected my furnishings with growing disbelief, winding up with the brass elephants tramping across the mantelpiece.

'Were these here when you came?'

'You think *I* brought them?'

He shook his straw-yellow head with reverence and awe. 'This house is weird!'

'Not weird; cut off by the tide.' When I was a child there were these last outposts of empire, with names like 'Lucknow' and 'Cawnpore', in every suburb from Brighton to Carlisle. Mr Pinner's finest hours were clearly spent in Simla, and a nameplate in curly poker-work hung over our front door.

He was a student of music – Charlie, not Mr Pinner – specifically of the cello, and he had won a three-month scholarship to study with some local lion who was now too ancient to go out to teach. His college had booked the room here on criteria of fiscal and geographic practicality: it was the most convenient room that Charlie could afford. He hadn't seen it until he had arrived an hour before.

'I'd sooner have walked further,' he confided, 'but what the hell, it's not worth moving again. Anyway, this may be the nearest I'll ever get to the Indian sub-continent.'

He may have said more than that: I didn't hear, I was out through the door like a slipped whippet in search of the elusive Mr Pinner.

I returned twenty minutes later to find Charlie curled up on my settee, his trainers doffed and his bare feet tucked up under him, reading a magazine with every sign of content-ment. He'd made a fresh pot of coffee and he uncurled long enough to pour it. 'You want to tell me again how this house isn't weird?'

'That wasn't the house being weird, that was me.'

It was what he'd said, that had finally made sense of the thing that had bothered me almost more than all the other things from the first moment I saw this house, this flat. I had *known* Luke had never chosen it, and when someone put the right question to him Mr Pinner was able to confirm that conviction. The room had been reserved for him, by telephone, by another man. Like Charlie, he'd had the place wished on him. Like Charlie, he hadn't intended staying long enough for it to matter. And he hadn't.

Mr Pinner didn't know who had phoned. The man claimed to be an old acquaintance from Skipley Horticultural Society, but Mr Pinner could place neither the name nor the voice. But he accepted the reservation in the name of Luke Shaw, because he saw no good reason not to, for one month because that was the minimum letting he made, and the money arrived by post a couple of days later under a local postmark. Luke turned up as expected, was polite and totally unforthcoming, and gave nobody a moment's concern until the third night when his radio blared out until after midnight. Mr Pinner had long since forgotten the name of the man who phoned, and it didn't seem to matter as it was certainly false. I said nothing but wondered if it had occurred to the respectable Mr Pinner that he had probably spoken with Luke's murderer.

Charlie didn't ask for one, being an easy-going member of a bohemian generation, but I felt some kind of explanation was called for. 'All the same, weird things have happened here. The man who had this room before me was murdered.'

'Perhaps he found the fusebox and had to be silenced.'

I'd come a long way in a week, but not so far I could take jokes about it. Sharp tears started to my eyes and thickened my voice. 'Charlie, he was my *friend* —'

He didn't leap to my side. He didn't stammer an apology. His seagreen eyes looked at me very straight and he said, 'The lucky sod.'

I didn't see too much of him for some time after that, although he was always around. I had reasons – both practical and fanciful – for not seeking his company. Whatever I had told Ben, I was still trying to resolve the enigma of Luke's death, and the success of my small inspiration about the room had fuelled a flagging enthusiasm by demonstrating again the advantage I had over official police enquiries by virtue of having known Luke so very well. Also, Ben himself was now occupying a fair amount of my time. It was still quite casual, with no suggestion or at that stage desire for emotional or other commitment; but we ended up seeing each other most evenings, for a drink or a bite of supper or just to talk. He wasn't and he never would be Luke, and the time might come when I'd stop wishing he was, but just for now he filled some of the empty spaces. Much of my time was accounted for.

The other reason, the fanciful one, for avoiding Charlie was based on what Harry Marsh had said, that Ben had laughed off. Marsh had anticipated some attempt by Luke's killers to keep an eye on me, at least until they were sure whether my morbid curiosity constituted any further threat to them. It was probably sheer coincidence that after months of standing empty the basement flat should find a tenant within days of my arrival, but coincidences have always made me uneasy and there was no reason in the circumstances not to play safe.

FIVE

It seemed to me I had two possible lines of enquiry that I was better placed to pursue than Chief Inspector Marsh. One was the house. My decision to live there, peculiar as it had been, had already been vindicated by Mr Pinner's information that would not otherwise have come out. But there was more to come. It had been important to someone's plan, whether or not murder was at that stage contemplated, to have Luke either in that house or in that immediate vicinity. There were other rooming houses in Skipley, which did not insist on a month's tenancy, so why pick one that did? Perhaps because of the privacy, the lack of regular contact, that implied. Perhaps they'd hoped the month would elapse before anyone found the body – for although I would have missed him before that, Skipley was about the last place on earth I would have searched for him, way down below the logging camps of British Columbia and the cathouses on Seventh Avenue, New York. At least I knew they existed.

But even if I accepted the house as seminal, I saw nowhere to follow the hypothesis at present. I couldn't believe the respectable Mr Pinner was involved – not because respectable people are incapable of crime, but because most of them are rotten at lying about it – and there was no one else to suspect. The importance of the house remained a secret among the people who chose it.

The other aspect of the affair that I was particularly

equipped to look into was this peculiar interest of Luke's in the renal system. It was difficult to see where the books I had found fitted in, harder to accept they could be irrelevant. Luke had gone to Skipley on the specific business which led to his death, and he had taken those books. They weren't light reading. Somehow they were important. They had to be. I needed to talk to somebody about kidneys, and happily I had the means to start at the top.

I hadn't seen Julian Barnes since that night in the Keys & Panther six months before, and until this business of the kidneys came up I hadn't thought about him either. Three phone calls tracked him down, to a private medical facility in Birmingham. The Schaefer Clinic was an impressive, glossy establishment set in landscaped gardens and extensively patronized by the foreign rich. Julian was their resident renal expert, and part of the territory was a research programme of which he was expansively, immodestly proud; not without reason.

He took me to lunch. We left my Citroen at the clinic and travelled in his enormous pearl-grey Mercedes, although the Deux Chevaux would have been easier to park and there was more chance of me leaving the restaurant fit to drive than of Julian doing so.

In the car, the effusive, well-meant, not particularly sincere greetings over, I looked curiously at the only living legend I knew. He looked good, guiding his big car confidently through the busy city streets. Prosperity had rounded some of the corners, filled out the angular and energetic frame, the lean and hungry face, and taken the chill out of the steely gaze which someone, in a memorable mixed metaphor, once described as reminiscent of a hatchet at feeding time. Success agreed with him, and even its camp-followers brought their own compensations. If he was beginning to look older – even in the last six months, or perhaps the bar lights had been kindly – it was also true that grey hair became him, and that the little lines gathering around his eyes only pointed up their sharp clear brilliance. A wolfish youth, he had matured into an undoubtedly handsome man.

Nor was there any sign yet that the flaming promise of his early career was burning down. If time had blunted the intensity it had also honed the intellect: an attractive shrewdness had supplanted some of the egotism of careless, which is to say uncaring, youth. He had become substantial, in every way – professionally, personally, in body and in mind. I hid a sudden rueful grin. This was how I had wanted him when he was youthful and visionary and arrogant; unfortunately, I too had matured and had somewhere mislaid the twenty-year-old face he had fallen for and the twenty-year-old body he had craved. Well-a-day; life never closes a window but what she also slams a door.

We were barely out of third gear before he moved on from the pleasantries of how-are-you, what-are-you-doing-now, do-you-ever-see-any-of-the-old-gang, to what he patently considered the only subject worth discussing: his research. He seemed to have forgotten that I asked to see him; at least he never asked why. He told me about his work and he made it last through to the dessert – when he had a miniscule portion of Stilton and I had a whacking great wodge of Black Forest Gateau – and I didn't begrudge him a moment of it. It was like hearing Fleming discourse on the possibility of penicillin. He was within striking distance of the medical breakthrough of the decade: the artificial implantable kidney.

He basked in my admiration that was by no means merely polite. 'It won't be today, of course, and it probably won't be this year, but I'll tell you this much, Clio. If a child of mine was facing renal dysfunction, I wouldn't be in too much of a hurry to get him a transplant.'

'You must have a lot of people holding their breath.'

His face fell a little. 'Time is the killer. Not disease. Diseases we can cure – now, or soon. But the cures always

44

come too late for somebody. However close I am to this, however quickly I get the answers, get through the clinical trials and get it into production, it's going to be too late for too many people. I'm going to lose patients because I didn't start six months earlier.'

'You're not God, Julian.' I leaned forward with a tiny smile. 'Still not, quite. Count the lives you save, not the deaths you can't prevent. How close are you?'

He held up a strong, delicate hand, candlelight barely showing between thumb and forefinger. 'That close. The technical problems are solved; only a few medical ones remain.'

I laughed. 'That's all?' People die of only a few medical problems every hour of every day. It's only a few medical problems that keep doctors in business. But I wished him luck. It would be an incredible achievement, opening the gate to all manner of artificial organs – a heart, a liver, a lung, maybe an eye – that could be built to a patient's require-ments, circumventing the whole business of tissue typing. It would mean implants being performed at the optimum time, not as and when someone with comparable D-tissue type dies in such a fashion as to leave his internal organs viable. It would remove the awful sickening strain of waiting for one person to die so another might have a chance of living, obviate the need to make distressing requests of newly bereaved relatives, most of all cut out half the guess-work – sorry, professional expertise – involved in matching an in-dividual living organ to an individual living recipient.

But all this was not why I had come. When he finally drew breath over the coffee I said, 'Julian, do you remember Luke Shaw?'

His eyebrows gathered. 'Shaw? – no – Yes. Wasn't that the young chap you introduced me to in that pub in London last September? I was down for a conference, and you two were celebrating – something or other?'

45

'My latest novel,' I supplied quietly.

'That's right. A rather nice lad, he seemed – in video or something, isn't he?'

'No, not quite. Actually, he's not in anything any more. He's dead.'

He listened, aghast, as I told the story. I hadn't intended to, only a few salient points, but once I had started and for as long as he listened I couldn't seem to stop. He listened like a professional, making it easy, and I didn't stop until I'd finished. Somewhere along the way he reached across the table and took my hand. It was a typical doctor's grasp, strong and cool. Despite being party to the mystique I drew comfort from it.

'It's monstrous,' he said when I was done.

'Oh yes,' I agreed. 'Also very strange, still. With all that we know of how he died, we have no idea why.'

'What can I do?'

'Almost certainly nothing,' I admitted. 'I didn't mean to lay all this on you. Only it occurred to me, after that night in the Keys & Panther, that if there was something Luke needed to know about kidneys he might approach you directly. I take it he didn't.'

Julian shook his head gravely. 'I'm sorry, Clio. I only met him the once. He seemed a decent lad. He was a bit special to you, wasn't he?'

'Yes.' I could think of nothing else to say, nothing else to ask him. It had been a long shot and it hadn't paid off, and it left me with nowhere to go. Still, we'd had a pleasant couple of hours and I didn't leave feeling I'd wasted my time.

Afterwards, back in the empire where sun never set, I remembered with a small pang of guilt that I hadn't asked to see round his department. I wasn't particularly anxious to – I was a doctor, not a medical scientist: however important his research was it was still technology until it became patient-applicable – but it struck me, belatedly, as rude not

46

to have shown a greater interest. I called him to thank him for the meal and ask if I could see round the clinic.

'Of course,' said Julian, after the briefest discernible pause. 'I'll enjoy showing it off to you.' But there was a note of reticence in his voice which his good manners did not wholly disguise.

'Unless this is a bad time for you?'

Relief, in the same fractional amount, replaced the reticence. 'As a matter of fact it is, rather. I've got the trustees from the funding organisation in this week – my grant's due for renewal. If we could leave it a few days – ?'

'Julian, you should have said earlier. I'm sure you had better things to do today than feed me and answer futile questions.'

'Man cannot live by grants alone,' he replied graciously. 'Anyway, I told them you were a brilliant biochemist of vital importance to the programme.' We both laughed. 'As to the questions, I'm only sorry I can't help. If you think of any more, don't hesitate to give me a call.'

'I shan't. Thanks, Julian.'

'And as soon as I have the chinless wonders off my back, and their money safely in my pocket, I'll lay on the grand tour.'

'I'll look forward to it.'

Funny old thing, life. A fortnight before Luke was the only real friend I had in the world. Now he was gone; but I was seeing Ben most days, I was fanning an old flame in the shape of Julian Barnes, and even the boy in the flat downstairs, who must have been twelve years my junior, seemed more attentive than simple neighbourliness would account for. There might have been a reason for that, of course.

I had to go down to London the next day to sign some papers with my publisher. When we were through with a conference which covered every contingency, including the improbable

47

one that someone might want to translate the latest epic into
Mandarin Chinese, I went round to my flat to check that it
hadn't been burgled, squatted in or made the latest battle-
field in the Middle Eastern war. I meant only to stick my
head in through the door, but as I did so home-sickness hit
me like a fist to the gut. All my possessions, all my comforts,
and a total lack of brass curios – even under a layer of dust it
looked like heaven. No elephants' feet, no mock-Turkey
carpets, no Mr Pinner being respectably elusive, no Charlie
Brown hanging ambiguously around; no atmosphere, no
history, no ghosts. I wanted to stay. I wanted very much to
throw up the whole silly crusade, have a hot soak in my own
bath, kick my shoes under my own bed and stay. I can't be
sure, but I think I just might have done if it hadn't been for
the phone call.

It was Miriam Frey, the personnel manager at ComIntel.
I'd met her a couple of times – a large, squarish, shrewdish
woman. I remembered rather liking her. I remembered that
Luke had, too.

She had been trying to get me for days, since Chief
Inspector Marsh told her about Luke. 'When it sank in I
cleared out his desk. There were some books and personal
things. Some of them have your name in them, and I imagine
he'd want you to have the others as well. I could have sent
them on but I didn't want them just arriving out of the blue. I
– I realise what this must have done to you. We're all so
sorry.'

I thanked her, meaning it. Hers was the first genuine
expression of condolence I had heard from anyone who knew
Luke. Julian Barnes, who met him once in a bar and thought
him a decent lad, hardly came into that category.

'I've been staying in the Midlands,' I explained. 'I'm
driving back this afternoon. I'll drop by you on my way, if
that's all right – I would like to have his things, if no one else
has any claim.'

48

'No one else has a better claim, anyway.' Miriam knew as well as I that since his mother died several years ago none of his family answered his letters; as if homosexuality was communicable by post.

She met me herself, which I appreciated because she had a big, busy job with the corporation. We walked along to Luke's office. 'He's going to be sadly missed,' she said, 'not just professionally. He made a lot of friends here.'

'He was happy here.' I looked along the white-walled corridors, the rows of identical small offices behind glass doors, about one in three enlivened by a potted plant. It was bright and pleasant but inexpressibly ordinary – not the environment for an aesthete. Yet it was true, he had been contented at ComIntel, partly because he enjoyed the work and was good at it, but mainly because of the acceptance he found among the people here. Some of them liked him and some of them didn't, but nobody gave him a hard time because of what he was. Miriam's comment and my response, equally platitudinous, were none the less both true. Harry Marsh, who didn't believe in the concept of happy homosexuality, could have learned something from seeing the people and the places where Luke's contentment was founded. After all, given abiding love, occasional romance, a good job, appreciative employers and amicable colleagues, why wouldn't a man be content?

It turned out Marsh had already paid a visit to ComIntel. I gathered he was a little surprised and more than a little impressed at the value the corporation placed on Luke's services. He had asked, as I should have thought to, what he had been working on recently, in case it was sensitive enough to warrant violent interruption, but though the firm had several government contracts and others of considerable commercial delicacy in hand, Luke's current assignment had been a new range of electronic games. It was a fun thing, bread-and-butter work that he'd taken on between more sophisticated projects, and apparently half the floor had got involved in devising Herculean labours for the neon characters. But I didn't believe Luke had died for a new generation of space invaders. Christ, I hoped not.

I asked if Miriam had noticed anything amiss in Luke's last days and weeks at ComIntel. She hesitated. 'Your policeman asked the same thing. I said Luke had seemed a bit funny. He didn't appear to find that particularly helpful.'

I could imagine. 'In what way funny?'

'Well – preoccupied. Not profoundly so, it didn't affect his work and the only time I asked about it he insisted there was nothing worrying him. I didn't give it much thought after that, until – But there was something.'

'When did you notice first?'

Miriam's strong brows drew together as she thought. 'Six weeks ago? Maybe two months. That was only when I realised there was something on his mind, of course. It may all have started a while before that.'

'And you've no idea what it was that was troubling him?'

She looked at me oddly and smiled. 'As a matter of fact, I thought I knew. I thought it was you.'

'Me?' My voice soared with incredulity. 'But – whatever – ?'

'Oh, nothing he said – I told you, he insisted there was no problem. I thought he was lying, but I also thought it was none of my business. It wasn't his work. You were the only person I could imagine him spending so much time worrying about. I thought something must have happened between you.'

It hadn't. Nothing had happened between us: so much nothing that I knew now I should have done something about it. Polite distance which was all I had been getting from him was never our scene. Like Miriam, I hadn't given it much thought, but I should have done. I might have saved him.

'I'd hardly seen him for three months,' I said. 'I just thought he was busy. I didn't even know he'd gone away until I was called up to some dreary bloody Midlands morgue to put a name on a body.' I stopped and caught my breath. Miriam was looking concerned. 'I'm all right. When did he tell you he was going?'

'He came to me on the Thursday and said he needed some leave right away. He thought he'd be back within a week. He worked over the weekend to clear his lines and left on the Monday. A week later we heard – well. But it wasn't like him, that. We didn't mind him taking time off if there was something he wanted to do, he usually had some owing, but it wasn't his habit to dash off like that. He was always thoroughly organised: we used to tease him about it. When he was taking leave he'd let me know weeks in advance. He took his commitments seriously. Whatever he needed the time for, it was urgent and it was important to him.'

It all pointed to a problem that had built up gradually, over as much as three or four months, and then suddenly come to a head. Why hadn't he told me about it? Perhaps Miriam was right, I thought slowly, letting the implications sink in. Perhaps, without my knowing it, Luke's problem had concerned me; or at least he had thought it did. Had he been trying to protect me from something? My palms went sweaty and my blood ran chill. Dear God, I thought, sitting down suddenly behind my friend's desk in his pot-plant jungle of an office, was the nightmare going to get worse before it got better? Was my amateur probing going to discover that in some terrible, freakish way Luke had died for *me*?

SIX

There were all sorts in the box of contents Miriam Frey made up for me. There were books of my own that Luke had borrowed so long ago I wouldn't have remembered them if he'd had the wit to remove my bookplates. There were several books of his, mostly technical volumes but interspersed endearingly with humour of the silliest, most juvenile kind. There were elegant little toys – a Newton's Cradle, a black and silver maze with a throbbing worm of mercury speeding down the channels, metal puzzles to challenge his deft fingers. There were glass and perspex paperweights: one could have been a Barracat, another looked as though a watch had exploded inside it. There was a clockwork camel. I almost expected to turn out a frog's skeleton next, or last season's champion conker.

And there were papers. Back in Simla I spread them around me in a circle on the mock-Turkey carpet and, handling them reverently, like treasures, I began working my way through.

The receipt, when I came to it, leapt up, waved its little papery arms in the air and yodelled 'Yoohoo, here I am!' in a thin treble voice. Or if it did not, I reacted as if it had. Currents like electricity coursed up my spine and set my neck hairs standing. Before I had recognised its specific significance I knew it was what I was looking for. It was dated three months back, it was from a bookseller and it was for quite a lot of money. It didn't detail the precise puchase, but knowing the cost of medical textbooks I was ready to hazard a guess. I fetched the two kidney books from the shelf and found where the price was printed on the jackets and added them up. It wasn't enough. So I went and got my copy of Barnes' *Causes & Treatments* that I'd brought from my flat, and I found the price on that and added it on.

'Just look what we have here,' I remarked very calmly to the leading elephant on the mantel piece, and the leading elephant agreed that what we had was a match.

So Luke had bought not two but three books – the Barnes and two others – which was almost odder than buying the others instead of the Barnes. The inference was that he had wanted to cross-check something. This was three months ago, back in London, so it had started before that. Then somehow the Barnes had become separated from the other books. He might have left it behind when he came to Skipley, but it made no sense: he had needed all three or he wouldn't have bought them, and I couldn't imagine a circumstance in which he might want both the other books but not the authoritative Barnes. The alternative hypothesis was much more tenable: that he had brought all three, because they were relevant to what he was doing here, and because it was relevant the men who came here to murder him took the Barnes away.

And the only conceivable reason for that was that they thought it could incriminate them. I hefted the great thing in my hand and turned to the back. There were 1,278 pages of closely packed type, and somewhere in there was the explanation: if I started reading now and didn't have to revise too much, I could have it by the time I was 83. I could then collect Harry Marsh from his old people's home, wheel him along to the appropriate graveyard and have him slap a warrant on the culprit's tombstone. There had to be an easier way.

I went out into the hall and picked up the phone. If anybody knew what was in the book its author should. I got halfway through the number and stopped, because a very nasty little thought hit me then.

The thought was, suppose it were not the contents of the book that the theft was meant to protect but the name on the cover?

It was absurd. However much I pussy-footed round it, if I admitted that as a serious possibility I was contemplating the idea that Julian Barnes was somehow involved in two murders. It was more than absurd, it was obscene, a vile slander on a man I had known and admired half my life. I felt ashamed of even thinking it. But when I dialled again I called not Julian but Ben Sawyer.

I don't know if Skipley was suffering a dearth of deaths that month, if they had a glut of pathologists, or if Ben's readiness to respond to my summonses left the morgue with a backlog of corpsicles that took months to defrost and autopsy when our little drama was done. Anyway, he was round at the flat inside twenty minutes, and arguing with me inside twenty-five.

'But you don't know he ever had the Barnes.'

'Jesus, Ben, it would be a bigger bloody coincidence if he didn't! You think he went to a medical bookseller and bought two obscure kidney books and another book or combination of books that just happened to cost the same as *Causes & Treatments*?'

'All right, maybe it was the Barnes,' Ben conceded. 'Any number of things could have happened to it. He could have lost it.'

'Lost it?' I was feeling badly about all this, Ben's witless nit-picking was doing little to make me feel better, and I made almost no effort at all to keep the derision out of my voice. 'When did you last lose a book? Especially a book you'd gone to a lot of trouble to find and paid a lot of money for. Luke never lost books.'

'He might have left it in London. Have you looked in his flat?'

'No –' I should have done, but I was back in Skipley before I found the receipt. 'Why would he buy it and leave it behind?'

'Why did he buy it at all? We don't know it has anything to do with this other – with his death.'

'Murder, Ben. He was murdered.'

We both stopped, more or less together, realising that we were shouting at each other. I sat down on the settee and Ben brought a chair from the dining-table and sat down facing me. I forced a smile and he took both my hands.

'All right, let's calm down and take this thing sensibly. You think there was a book and it's important that it's missing. I'll accept you could be right if you'll accept you could be wrong. Deal?'

I closed my eyes for a moment to will my racing nerves to steady. 'It's a deal.' I grinned weakly and shook his hands. 'Okay, it's a deal.'

'Good.' Ben smiled too, with warmth and concern but also with a relief he could not disguise. He had thought I was on the brink of hysteria. He was wrong about that. The brink of hysteria was where I'd lived for a week after it happened, I knew it well, but I had not lost my balance then and I knew, even if it didn't show, that my control and stability had been improving since. I still felt bitter rage and grief, but these were normal reactions to an abnormal situation – there was nothing hysterical about them. Anyone who thought I was still behaving oddly hadn't known me before.

Ben said, 'Supposing for the moment it was the Barnes and it was stolen. What's your thinking on that?'

That was the spot, all right, and he'd put me on it, and he wasn't going to help me out by coming up with the same idea himself. It was decision time. If I said what I was thinking –

55

no, not even thinking, what my nasty little mind had come up with in an unguarded moment when I had let it off the leash – there would be no going back. You can't shove all the hassle back inside Pandora's box: wrong or improbably right, the consequences of an allegation like that would stretch beyond any horizon I could see. But if I didn't say it – now, to a friend, in answer to a direct question – I might as well close the whole sordid chapter and go home, because if I didn't even dare contemplate the possibility I had no right to be muddying the waters for those who would.

I did not relish Ben's response to what, however carefully I worded it, could only sound like vicious, unsubstantiated melodrama. But even more I dreaded the disgust and self-loathing I should feel if I funked the issue for fear of what anyone else might think. I wasn't about to accuse Julian Barnes of anything. I didn't believe he was responsible for Luke's death. I didn't believe Luke could have known enough about him to drive a man everyone agreed was a brilliant medical scientist – potential Nobel Prize material: he was that good – to murder. But Julian was a doctor, he was a kidney expert, his book was somehow tied up in all of this, and if unheard-of bloody Skipley was not exactly on his doorstep it was a lot closer to the Schaefer Clinic than it was to London. When it was all added up it was nowhere near enough to justify an accusation. But it was too much to dismiss.

I said, 'I see two possibilities. No, three – the third is that I'm quite wrong and the book really is irrelevant, but I don't think so. Of the others, the first is that *Causes & Treatments* confirmed some suspicion Luke had about something – something illegal, presumably, or at least unsavoury. He was lured here or came here to confront the person he suspected, and the bastard killed him and took the evidence.'

But Julian's book wasn't a new publication: it had been a standard work of reference for most of a decade. Admittedly it had been updated by several revisions, but if it contained anything incriminating or controversial it would have been discovered long enough since, and by a doctor, not an electronics wizard.

'And the second?' Ben said quietly.

'That Barnes himself is in some way implicated, and the book was removed so that no link between Julian and Luke would survive Luke's supposed suicide.' I said it quite flatly and without stumbling, and when it was out I waited for the expected storm with an unlooked-for lightness of spirit.

Ben had gone the colour of parchment. His skin seemed to have sagged and his warm eyes were hollow with shadows. He said sickly, 'Clio, you *can't* think Julian Barnes – a man like that, a remarkable respected man – was responsible for what happened to Luke.'

It went against everything he had been taught and believed in: the Hippocratic Oath, the exercise of skill and devotion in the preservation of human life, the unspoken, unsuspected, very deep love of a doctor for the people in his charge – as a principle if not as individuals. But there is no logical reason to assume that doctors are more intrinsically good than engineers, say, or grocers. Some measure up to the highest standard; most don't; and every so often you get a Crippen. And when you do, he has a better chance of getting away with his murders than a grocer.

But it wasn't Crippen we were talking about, it was Julian Barnes; not a grim shadow caught by history's spotlight in a single terrible deed but a man I knew, a man I liked; a friend.

Understanding hit me like Greek fire, withering. I felt myself go white; my voice dropped to a reedy whisper. 'The man's my friend. That's why Luke kept his suspicions to himself – until he was sure, and then it was too late.'

In the profound silence of a grief that was no longer to do with Luke alone we stared at one another over our joined hands; I don't know how long for. We had turned over the pebbles until we found something horrid, and now the ugliness reflected back on us. At length, still in silence, Ben rose and left the flat. He came back with a bottle of whisky from which he dumped liberal measures into two glasses. He threw his back with determination and some distaste, and stood over me while I sank mine.

'All right. Where do we go from here?'

I could have kissed him, or wept or something. Not because he believed me – he seemed still to baulk at that final admission of the obscenity – but because of that lovely word 'we'. It was getting complicated and nasty, on a personal rather than purely intellectual hands-in-the-air, Oh-how-awful level, and by that one word he had allied himself with my battle instead of leaving me to fight alone. That loyalty came at a time when I needed support more than I needed help and I appreciated it deeply.

I said, 'Police, I suppose,' without any great enthusiasm.

The prospect of taking my theory to Chief Inspector Marsh inspired no greater happiness in Ben than it did in me. 'I suppose we've no choice,' he agreed glumly.

'We've no evidence either. He'll throw us out on our ear again.'

'But if you can show – ?'

'What can I show him? I *know*, damn it, but what can I prove?' Frustration tore at my throat like claws. 'I know how Luke died, I know something of why, God help me I even know who did it – but if I persuaded them to pick him up today he'd walk free tomorrow. It takes more than smart theories to topple gods, Ben, it takes irrefutable bloody proof and I haven't got any. Listen, if I went to Marsh and told him it was you, he might consider my intuition excuse enough for a discreet investigation. If I tell him it's Barnes, it'll be like trying to get St Paul demoted on the strength of something Mary Magdalen once said to Judas Iscariot. I don't want him to get away with this, Ben. I want him nailed.'

'Harry Marsh isn't a bad policeman,' he argued weakly. 'If you put your cards on the table – '

'He'd have me certified. He's already half convinced I'm crazy. If I told him Julian Barnes of the Schaefer Clinic was implicated in the murder of a homosexual and a teenage dropout, he'd be sure of it. Even if he believed me, I don't think he'd know what to do about it. If this thing involves Julian Barnes and Luke Shaw, it's about medical science of a particularly advanced variety and quite possibly electronics too. I doubt the police manual has much to say on either subject. Marsh is no match for the man who killed Luke – he'd be out of his depth.'

'There are experts available to the police,' said Ben with a ghost of a smile. 'Witness me.'

I managed a grin in reply. 'Yeah. But you're part of the system. Any outside help he needs he has to ask for, and before he'll ask for it he has to accept there's good cause. You know him better than me: can you see him applying for a boffin to solve his murders for him?' I couldn't, and neither could Ben, a fact which he conveyed with a small, almost apologetic grimace like a facial shrug. I nodded grimly. 'Just so. And if I'm wrong there are no such implications anyway, just a grubby little killing he can handle perfectly well on his own. That's what he wants it to be, and he won't give that up until he's made to. Hell, he was all for skimping the post-mortem because he thought he knew what it would show. He's about as much chance of finding his way through something this complicated as I have of assembling a nuclear submarine from a construction kit.'

I realised, belatedly I think, that Ben was regarding me oddly. He was frowning and his eyes were disturbed. 'Clio – exactly what are you suggesting?'

It was a good and pertinent question for which I had no immediate answer. I didn't know what I was suggesting – keeping my suspicions from Chief Inspector Marsh, taking them to someone else, acting on them myself – I hadn't been thinking in those terms. But I did so now, and felt my body respond with a quickening in the veins: adrenalin, born of the unholy union of fear and anticipation. Because what I found when I confronted my jumbled emotions and made them pick sides was that I was not prepared to back down. I wanted Luke's murderer enough to take the consequences of going after him, and I suddenly knew how to do that too. The champagne sensation in my blood was the thrill of commitment, reinforced by the irrational sense of release that comes of burning boats. If I wasn't going back, I knew where I was going instead.

I drew a deep breath and clenched my fingers into fists and, keeping my voice deliberately flat so that the adrenalin wouldn't reverberate and make me sound drunk or witless, I said, 'I'll hand this over to Marsh when I have the evidence to make him take action and not before. It needn't be too much – just something concrete to support what I say. Once he accepts that Julian Barnes could be involved he'll be quick enough to ask for help – it'll be too big for him not to, like anyone else if it comes to a straight choice he'll put his career before his dignity. I only have to present him with that choice. I need something to slap on his desk beside my theories and intuition.'

I couldn't have said what. But I was quite sure in my own mind that the evidence I sought existed somewhere, in some form. It had to. Julian Barnes was a clever man by any standard, but he had made three bad mistakes. The first put Luke on to him more than three months ago. I didn't know what that was yet. The second – using a ruined child as a prop in a scenario intended to discredit Luke and have his death pigeon-holed – enabled me to show the probability of murder, subsequently and perhaps consequently confirmed by Ben's autopsy. The third was the removal of his own book from Luke's shelves, when its absence implied so much more than its presence and anyway that whole vital aspect could have been covered up if he'd thought to take the other two as well.

A man who makes three bad mistakes in as many months will probably make more. Certainly he cannot be considered invulnerable. That thought alone was like a tonic. Even if I was not clever enough to discover his Achilles heel, if I was dogged enough, if I stayed close to the man, if I haunted his every move, sooner or later it would let him down and I would know. Then it would be a race as to whether I got to Chief Inspector Marsh first or Julian Barnes got to me.

SEVEN

Some of the groundwork we could do without probing much deeper than the level of public knowledge. Ben undertook to investigate the financial arrangements at the Schaefer Clinic, particularly how the research there was funded. I wanted to know who provided the money, on what basis, and whether the source was reputable. I also wanted to know if it was true that Julian's grant was up for renewal and assessors from the funding trust had indeed spent the week at his laboratory.

My task was to discover whether the Barnes AIK belonged in the same world as Luke Shaw and his electronic children. If it did there was a connection: tenuous perhaps, but something to follow up. If it didn't, if the design was based on purely mechanical filters, then I had no more idea why Luke had died than Chief Inspector Marsh. And if I didn't know why, I could be wrong about who. So I approached the inquiry with trepidation and an equal balance of dread that I was wrong, in which case I wouldn't know where to turn next, and that I was right, in which case I had to track Luke through a minefield of technologies I only marginally understood in order to discover what he had discovered. It would also be preferable if, in reaching the same conclusion, I could avoid meeting the same end.

Biomedical engineering is a highly specialised field. The average GP would not be familiar with its intricacies, would count himself lucky to know someone who understood it in any detail, and for obvious reasons my one knowledgeable friend was out as a source of information. Instead I opted for a pincer movement on the truth: I directed inquiries to the renal department of my old hospital, which might have been less classy than the Schaefer Clinic but had a good record for sending patients home both physically and financially intact; and also to Miriam Frey at ComIntel, asking if either Luke himself or anyone else there had been working on biomedical systems. I appreciated that she would be professionally inhibited from disclosing much about either the product, if there was one, or the client, but in all the circumstances I thought she'd find a way of tipping me off if there had been such a project. I phrased my query carefully and specifically: if the answer was no that was what she'd say, and if she said she was not at liberty to discuss it the answer was yes.

Ben's results came through quicker than mine. Money to set up the Schaefer Clinic had come from, and the profits now went to, an American source which owned several similar establishments in the States. They were uncompromisingly commercial in approach, and in consequence devastatingly successful, but no shadow of impropriety attended the operation. The clinics provided a product – mostly in the nature of 20,000-mile services for those who could afford and wanted to treat their bodies like sports cars – to meet a demand from a lot of vain, self-indulgent people and quite a few desperate ones literally sick of waiting for the National Health Service, and if it wasn't my idea of medicine it was nobody's idea of crime.

The clinic provided research facilities as part of Julian's contract, but most of the money involved came from a five-year grant awarded by an international trust. It was given for his work on the AIK, and it was indeed up for renewal. Four sombre men with accents were staying at a Birmingham hotel convenient to the clinic. The organisation was as reputable as the Bank of England and quite possibly richer. There was no room for speculation there.

The first of my enquiries to be favoured with a response was that to Miriam. It was direct, unambiguous and negative. No one at ComIntel had ever worked on a project for the Schaefer Clinic; no one there had worked on an artificial kidney for anyone; Luke had done no medical work, and though there had been such projects during the period of his employment none was more recent than nine months ago and none had any apparent relevance to my particular field of interest. It wasn't the answer I wanted, but I couldn't blame Miriam for short-changing me. You can hardly say no more comprehensively than that.

Then fragments of information began trickling in from former hospital colleagues. I got phone calls from people I hadn't seen or thought of in years. I got a couple of fairly lengthy letters, a surprising proposition, and from an anaesthetist a manilla envelope thick with papers. I remembered him: his young son was down to one rather dodgy kidney and his interest was therefore more personal than professional. He had photo-copied for me an obviously dog-eared, much-thumbed publication by Barnes on the search for the AIK. It was several years old, drafted probably while he was still looking for funding and before his own research got important and secret. That made it perhaps the last thing he wrote in the spirit of shared knowledge. After this, soon after, the money came through, the thing got viable and the wraps went on. The publication was a kind of time capsule.

Reading it I experienced that singular thrill of quiet triumph, that feeling of absolutely rightness, when you know – instinctively or intuitively, because sense has little to do with it and science nothing at all – that you're on the brink of something big, that you're right and it's right and the stars are right and this time you just can't help but make it good; a lightness, a brightness, an intoxication, when you feel so bloody clever you imagine the rest of the world must see it, like a halo round your admirable head.

The sort of feeling a man would get who, after years of study and work and mind-breaking research and heart-breaking disappointment, suddenly made the final connection, the last imaginative leap that put the artificial implantable kidney within his grasp. It was a staggering thing – a golden fleece, a Holy Grail – and with the sharpened vision of my own small victory I could see how achieving it could turn a modest man arrogant and an arrogant man into a Caesar. A man like that would be proud enough to believe in the importance of defending his own reputation, and strong enough to do it. A man like that could kill rather than fail. Like many another before him, Luke had been sacrificed to a clever man's aspiration to divinity.

None of this was in the paper, except perhaps the sense of destiny. The text had been written by the Julian Barnes I used to know: the brash one, whose egotism I had disliked, whose dynamic single-mindedness I had mistrusted, whose incisive, imaginative, original mind I had recognised as the nearest thing to genius I was ever likely to know. All my friends were medical types then, and I and all of us accepted Julian as the one of our number who would make his name. It was inconceivable that his potential would not be realised. If anyone had suggested that it would be realised over the body of a murdered innocent like Luke Shaw I'd have referred him to Psychiatry and given him the night number; and I would have been right. The Julian Barnes of those heady, heartless days was many things – ambitious, impatient, insensitive, ruthless – but he would never have sunk that low: not only because we were newly weaned on the sanctity of human life, but because he would have despised to flaw the perfect brilliance of his beckoning career with something so crude. He was genuinely devoted to his science, serving it not only with skill and great promise but with honesty, with integrity. He never lowered his standards to cheat. That was something new, something he had learned, and he had learned it in the rich years since he wrote the AIK paper.

It was less a publication of findings than a statement of intent. He began by describing the nature and scale of the problem: the incidence of renal failure, the difficulties of getting donor organs, the obstacles to finding a sufficiently perfect match, the perpetual battle against rejection. He tabulated the demand on fiscal and medical resources made by dialysis machines, and castigated in coldly clinical terms which did nothing to disguise the fury behind them the failure of the British medical system to provide adequate treatment facilities. The international league-table showed that a duff Swiss kidney was more than twice as likely to receive treatment, an Israeli one nearly twice as likely, and thirteen others including Italian, Spanish and Cypriot in a better position than a British kidney on the blink.

Even those patients who got dialiysis hadn't too much to celebrate. The programme was a massive intrusion into any kind of normal life, and offered at best only a holding measure. Dialysis machines stopped patients dying: they didn't make them well.

Dialysis two or three times a week, for eight or ten hours at a time, cleans from the blood those waste products which are the province of the functioning kidney, which if left to their own devices build up to toxic and ultimately lethal proportions. But it's like pumping air into a tyre with a slow leak: the moment you stop, you begin losing way. The impurities mount, making the patient feel unwell, until he goes back on the machine; and even then he can't win, because dialysis also tends to remove useful hormones and vitamins. The dialysis machine was a marvellous invention. It saves lives on a daily basis. But it's not the last word to be said on the subject.

The ideal artificial kidney would operate like the original model: often imitated, never bettered, nobbling the blood's impurities as they drift along rather than doing a spring-clean twice a week. What kidney patients, doctors, economists and everybody else really wanted and what Julian Barnes was working on, was a personal dialysis machine, small enough to be portable, so it could be slow enough to spend all week filtering a week's worth of toxicity, which in turn would allow it to be simple enough that one could be provided for every patient and the attendance of highly trained staff would be unnecessary. It would be the equivalent of taking a patient off a heart-lung machine and giving him a pace-maker.

The AIK concept became feasible if equipment the size of a bookcase could be miniaturised to something the size of a pocket Bible. And the whole business of miniaturisation, given a push-start by the small Japanese gentlemen and their even smaller transistors, went into overdrive with the development of the microprocessor industry. The time was ripe for a man with the skill, the imagination, and the technological and financial backing, to present the waiting world with the personalised U-Tote-It artificial kidney.

That was the prize. That – and the little things that would go with it: the little bit of prestige, for instance, and the little bit of money – was what Julian Barnes was after, that he was within a stone's throw (comparatively speaking: a year or two is budgie seed to medical science) of achieving, and which in some extraordinary way Luke had come to threaten. And which, I added parenthetically, because I didn't want to forget it in the thrill of the chase, I now threatened too.

The paper was written on the basis of principles and preliminary work, predating as it did the current research at the Schaefer Clinic. But if microprocessors were indeed the key to the AIK, it was coming palpably close to Luke's area of excellence. If Julian's research was in some way fraudulent and Luke had caught him out, this was where it happened. I wished to God it was an area in which I had some competence myself.

Such as it was, both circumstantial and compelling, I laid the evidence before Ben when he came round that evening. He studied the papers in silence, his face still, only the familiar perplexed frown deepening between his eyebrows. When at last he looked up his eyes were dark, full of apprehension and grief. I felt contradictory stabs of satisfaction and regret. I needed him on my side, I needed him to believe. For his own safety, not to mention mine, he had to understand what Barnes was and was capable of. But I was deeply sorry to have destroyed his faith. He was a simple man, Ben Sawyer, intelligent but not intellectual. He lived in a world painted in primary colours, in which heroes wore white, villains wore black and doctors squandered their own health ministering to the needs of others before being pressed to a well-earned retirement (country cottage, roses round the door, trout stream, occasional requests for help from respectful young replacement) by a grateful community. Doctors did not, in this bright and sunny land, go round murdering people, for money or reputation or any of the other sordid considerations that tempt ordinary mortals. Finding that they sometimes did, even the best and cleverest of them, knocked the foundations from under all his life that he had built. He was shattered and ashamed; and convinced.

I caught his hurt eyes and made him look at me. 'We're agreed, then?' He nodded mutely. It wasn't enough: I wanted it stated, out in the open where it couldn't later be forgotten or put discreetly to one side. I wanted a commitment. 'It was Barnes. Julian Barnes killed Luke, because something Luke knew threatened his project, and he killed the boy to make it look authentic.'

'Yes,' whispered Ben. 'Dear God, that's how it looks.'

'And and I want him, Ben. I want him.'

That startled him, more than all the rest. 'Clio – he'll

68

crucify you!'

'I don't doubt he'll try.'

'Try?' His voice rose to a shaky plaint. 'He's killed two people already: now isn't the moment for second thoughts. If he guesses what you know – '

'He won't have to guess. I intend to tell him.'

Ben looked he'd been hit in the gut with a sack full of gold dust. I swear his eyes spun. He looked as if he was about to say half a dozen different things. Finally he blinked, shook his head and said, quite flatly, 'I don't understand you.'

I began methodically sorting the papers on the table. It gave me something to do with my hands as well as a rhythm to order my thoughts. It also, of course, cleared a place for supper. I kept my tone equally prosaic. 'Julian Barnes murdered my friend. I want him to pay for that. The police won't take me seriously as it is. If I tell them that one of the lions of modern medicine murdered a queer and a drop-out to protect some awful secret about a project that could win him the Nobel prize, they'll have me studying ink-blots down the local funny farm before you can say Artificial Implanatable Kidney.

'Julian Barnes has done well for himself. He's made money, but more importantly he's made the kind of reputation for himself that will protect him against fire, flood and all other acts of God including vengeful women. He's a wealthy, respectable doctor working for a wealthier, respectable organisation. You can't topple institutions with the same doubts, suspicions and persistence you use to nobble ordinary crooks. You can't even topple them with truth – not in this country, Watergate would have made Nixon a fortune in libel damages if it had happened here. It takes proof: hard, unassailable proof, the kind you'd expect the police to get except that to get it they have to look and they won't look while they consider Barnes' reputation more substantial than my claims.

69

'But there's something: some evidence, some chink in the armour, something – Luke found it or he'd be alive now. I don't know what it is. But Julian does: you can be sure he found out before making free with the razor and the Berber cushion. So maybe I don't have to find out what Luke knew, only persuade Julian that I have. If the cat jumps he may give me all the proof I need.'

'Assuming,' Ben said tightly, 'you're in any state to use it.'

'That is,' I admitted, 'seminal to my planning. You can help there, if you will.'

That offended him. He read into it more than just my desire not to take him for granted, or make grand gestures with anybody's hide but mine. He thought his courage was at issue, or his manhood or something. The urge to make a grand gesture of his own warred in him with realism. 'Of course I will. But Clio, my efforts notwithstanding, if you get us into a confrontation with a man who has already killed, who has his back against the wall, who has nothing to lose and everything to gain, we're going to end up queueing for harp lessons on the same cloud as your friend.'

I grinned fiercely. 'Don't worry, I know both our limitations. It's not so much a bodyguard I'm after as a witness: an insurance policy, a whistle-blower, a sealed envelope Julian may guess I've arranged to have opened in the event of my death but the nature and whereabouts of which he won't know anything about. As long as we keep you two apart you should be safe enough, and if you are I am too. Christ!' I added abruptly, thinking of Charlie.

'Now what?'

'The boy downstairs. I think he may be part of this. He's seen you, Ben. He must have seen you coming here.'

'You think he's working for Barnes – some sort of spy? Why do you think that?'

'Only because he arrived at a highly opportune moment if Julian did want someone in here keeping an eye on me. He's

70

supposed to be studying music but he always seems to be hanging around. He's seen you – '

'Listen,' Ben said firmly, taking my hands. The despair and the brief anger had lapped from his eyes, to be replaced by an unexpected and reassuring authority. 'Even if he is spying for Barnes, and even if he has seen me, what good will it do him? He doesn't know my name, or where I work or what I do. He doesn't know that I have any interest in Luke's death. We might be the most casual of acquaintances. He can't do a positive vetting on everyone you meet in Skipley. Perhaps we should be more careful. But I don't think you need worry about every layabout between here and the Bull Ring: there are far too many for them all to be Barnes' men.'

He was right, of course. Charlie might have been planted on me, but probably he was exactly what he claimed and appeared. The time was coming when Julian Barnes would feel sufficiently threatened by my presence in his part of the world that he might try to monitor my activities, but that time was not yet. And it would be a time of my choosing, not his, because it would begin when I walked into his office and gave notice of my intention to break him.

ONE

I walked into his office with no invitation, no warning, no announcement, only a brief barbed smile at his receptionist which could not honestly have been described as threatening but which would have made Torquemada get on with what he was doing.

I had hoped to find his important guests with him, but in that I was disappointed. But he was not alone. My unheralded arrival brought them lurching to their feet: two young stalwarts of the medical industry in white coats left casually ajar to show the expensive threads beneath. Patients of the Schaefer Clinic were clearly better mannered than to bleed on their physicians.

I knew them; not their faces or their names, but more important things about them. They came of medical families. They had qualified at good medical schools. They had been average students, inclined to frivolity, but anchormen of their respective rugby teams. They had drunk, and wenched, and been admired, a little more than was good for them. They had qualified adequately rather than impressively, and had walked straight into two of the best jobs going primarily because they or their fathers knew somebody who knew somebody. One would specialise in facelifts and breast remodelling and the other in athletics injuries, and they would stay at the Clinic until they received irresistibly lucrative offers of their own departments in similar establishments or joined partnerships in the Dowager Duchess belt. Oh, and one other thing. They murdered Luke.

They were both big. One was only slightly smaller than Wales. They didn't look particularly evil; callous, perhaps, when they were less worried than they were at this moment. There was a certain florid element in their make-up, in style as in complexion, that did not bespeak an overwhelming sensitivity: I wouldn't have put my breasts or cartilages in their hands, or my bank account or used car either, but that was a personal view. Others might be attracted by that same air of rugged, reckless youth, and when they stopped gulping at me like affronted goldfish and said something I did not doubt but that the accents would be wonderful.

But I knew their secret – intuitively, I suppose, they weren't wearing Murderer lapel badges and Julian Barnes would have God knows how many innocent people through his office in the course of a week, but I knew them all right. In the same way it took only that first startled look for them to know me, who I was and why I was there. At least it saved time on the introductions.

Julian seemed to feel it incumbent upon him to make some anyway. He had shot from his seat a little like Columbine from a circus cannon at the rape of his privacy, but he'd had more practice than his associates at disguising his feelings. He quickly translated his abrupt and angry elevation into an urbane gesture of welcome, thrusting his arm across his broad desk towards me and wreathing his handsome face with a friendly, kindly, sincere smile of the kind only a doctor in private practice can conjure. The voice was hearty and deckle-edged with pleasure.

'Why, Clio! What a delightful surprise. I wasn't expecting you. Oh dear.' Well-feigned contrition washed through his demeanour. 'Should I have been?'

I considered that for a moment, then nodded. 'Yes, I rather think you should.'

'Then I am foolish as well as remiss,' he said gallantly, flashing the handsome smile round the room, 'spending with these ne'erdowells time which I should have spent with you. I don't think you've met my colleagues, have you? – John Harwich, Peter Chandos: Doctor Clio Rees. Gentlemen, I wonder – ?'

The staggered look on their two big faces was yielding to a sullen watchfulness that was hardly more appropriate if all I had walked in on was a medical conference. They hadn't been discussing medicine, or a patient – or perhaps they called them clients. Unless they had a whole fund of guilty secrets and skeletons jostling for elbow-room in every cupboard, they had been talking about Luke. And me? – maybe; and maybe what to do if I should come calling. A small part of me wanted to scream but most of me was cool, deathly cool, because I wouldn't have come this far if my desire to repay them had not outweighed my fear.

I said negligently, 'Let them stay. This concerns all of you.'

The larger of the two, the one qualifying for independent nationhood and his own TV channel, was Chandos. Thinking himself behind my line of sight he threw Barnes a fast look electric with significance which Julian was far too experienced a dissembler to acknowledge. His eyes were firmly on me. His voice dropped a tone and he managed to sound mildly offended. 'Clio, I'm sorry if I've upset you, but if you've come here to give me a dressing down I'm sure you won't want to embarrass members of my staff by doing it in front of them.' His imperious gaze, as palely blue as the depths of a good diamond, left my face for an instant and he nodded at the door. The large young men were on the far side of it before I could intervene.

I shrugged. 'You can convey the salient points to them later.'

Julian's manner was subtly changing. He settled back in

his chair, weighing me up. He knew that I knew something, but not how much; he knew that I wanted something, but not what. The affability, the welcome and the injured dignity had all outlived their usefulness: I saw them slowly soften, dissolve and leech away. What remained was colder, harder, aware − sharply intelligent, a sudden mirror-image in a mature man's smooth face of the fierce implacable drive of ruthless youth. I remembered that look, the brilliance and the arrogance it sprang from, and the dazzling future it had seemed to promise when we were both little more than children.

It was eerie, that, like looking at one thing through a window and suddenly seeing another thing reflected in the glass. It was also rather frightening, because I had thought the man who was my enemy had murdered, long before he murdered Luke, that earlier man who had been my friend. If Julian Barnes of the infinite promise had been not destroyed but absorbed, I had to deal with not only a greedy and arrogant man but one of incisive intellect, sweeping vision, vaulting ambition and the kind of impatience that makes people run on escalators. If the man I now confronted was the product not of revolution but of evolution, no usurper but the legimiate heir of all those advantages and aspirations, he was twice the adversary I was prepared for.

He had been many things when I knew him first but his saving grace had always been his honesty. If it had its roots, as I suspected, in disdain for the weakness of falsehood rather than a scrupulous regard for the truth, it was still a powerful constraint on a man who had enough talent to pick and choose among the social laws imposed on us more ordinary mortals. If that honesty was the only casualty of his success, there was little room for hoping that the new polished facade hid a mentality worn similarly smooth by the intervening years. The polish went on with the second-mortgage suit and the hand made shoes: beneath it the intellect was as sharp as ever. If I underestimated him for a moment I would be lost.

He said quietly, 'Very well, Clio. Do you want to tell me what this is all about?'

I smiled. 'All right, Julian. Just for the record and so there'll be no misunderstandings later, it's about Luke Shaw. He was that rather nice lad who wasn't exactly in video, and who bled his life away in a grotty bed-sitter light-years from home because he was unfortunate enough to stumble on the truth about you.

'I can't know, of course,' I went on, settling into my stride, finding enough detachment to be grateful that anger and vengeance had turned my voice to steel rather than a whinge, 'not having been there, but it's my guess that your tame gorillas who just left held him down while you stifled the fight out of him, and went on holding him after you opened his wrists. It must have worked wonders for your ego that it took the three of you to deal with someone Luke's size.

'And the boy, of course; but I don't suppose he gave you much trouble, not once you'd fixed him up. Did he thank you, Julian? I bet he did. That was good stuff you gave him, better than he could afford. But Luke knew you weren't there for a party, and all three of you couldn't keep him from crying out. What would you have done if someone had come: blown the whole bloody building up?'

We stared at each other in the sudden silence, shocked but perhaps also a little relieved at having the thing so unequivocally out in the open. I was leaning on my fists on his desk, the knuckles gone bone-white against the mahogany plain, and I waited breathing softly to see what he would say.

He must have considered prevarication, must have decided it was too late for that. He said, 'I didn't want this, Clio. I never intended – '

I laughed in his face, savage with incredulity. 'Never intended to kill him? You only meant to bleed him a little bit, like a goddamn Masai cow?'

76

Across the desk he rose again, fluid with anger, unconsciously echoing my bellicose stance so that we must have resembled a pair of belligerent book-ends eyeballing one another. Julian said forcefully, 'He just kept coming.'

He just kept coming. Little Luke, who found his closest friend's friend was up to his hairline in deceit and would neither blow the whistle nor back down until he understood just where the implications began and ended. And if he'd found that I was indeed involved, of my own free will, what would he have done then? Nothing, I think, because although he abhorred all forms of cheating and exploitation and injustice, he loved me more than he hated them. But it would have broken his heart. Dear God, I hoped he understood before they killed him that I knew nothing of events at the Schaefer Clinic. He should have learnt that much: if he knew enough to make him dangerous, surely he knew that? Poor Luke, cat-curious, pathologically incapable of turning a blind eye, too stubborn in his doe-eyed gentleness ever to walk away. He just kept coming.

I sat down and so did Julian, watching me warily. I said, 'I suppose you tried to warn him off?'

'Of course. Not at first,' he explained carefully. It was as if he was describing the course of a disease to me. 'At first I did nothing. I thought he'd lose interest or decide he was mistaken or give up – everything. He had nothing to go on. One careless word, that was all, and he guessed two months before I did that we'd taken a wrong turn with the research.' A note of desperation had invaded his cultured voice. Despite what he had done, incredibly he saw himself as the victim in the piece. He forced a bitter laugh. 'And they say God has no sense of humour. If that young man had been working for me, the problem would not have arisen; and if I'd never met him I could have contained it until my grant was safe and then solved it in my own good time. As it was, the whole programme was at risk. Clio, the whole programme:

years of work, work that's going to save countless lives.' His eyes on my face suddenly sharpened. 'You do know what this is all about?'

'The AIK.'

'The AIK,' he echoed. He shook his head. 'It sounds like nothing when you say it like that. And you know too that when you leave here I shall deny this conversation ever took place. So far as the world will know and believe, you'll be a spurned woman from my mis-spent youth come back to haunt my prosperous middle-age.'

I had to grin, if sourly. Oh yes, the man I remembered was here yet. And if it came to his word against mine, Marsh for one would take his. Damn it, in other circumstances so would I have done. I nodded. 'I know that.'

He looked puzzled. 'Then why are you here?'

I gave him two reasons, and while both of them contained elements of truth neither was wholly honest. 'I wanted to hear your account. I wanted to know if you had any justification at all for what you did. Also, I wanted you to know that you hadn't got away with it.'

Julian regarded me speculatively. 'Are you threatening me, Clio?'

'Well, let's call it a threat,' I offered magnanimously.

He chuckled appreciatively. 'You always did have more courage than anyone we knew.'

'Yes, but not that much. I've taken out insurance against you, Julian. You'll leave me alone because everything I know and everything I suspect I have told to someone else – someone you don't know, never will know, couldn't find if you did – and though, alive, I can't prove any of it, if something unfortunate happens to me the police will have no option but to look into it. You need me alive. Your reputation wouldn't save you if your name was linked with three murders.'

He said softly, 'No. They know nothing of this?'

'I haven't spoken to them since I realised it was you.'

'Thank you for that.'

'Don't thank me. Make me understand, if you can. Give me some reason to protect you. Tell me what happened, and why.'

Julian raised one laconic eyebrow. 'It is a complete fallacy that the perpetrators of evil deeds feel the desire to confess.'

'It's not a confession I'm after. I know you're guilty: what I want to know is why.' My lips curled at a sudden thought. 'I'm not wired for sound, if that's what's bothering you. You can frisk me if you like.'

The bastard did.

It had begun, as I had come to fear, that night in the Keys & Panther, and it had happened because I had introduced two men who would never otherwise had met. I tried to remember what we had discussed and met a blank: just woolly half-memories of casual banter, some of it friendly, some of it edged, interspersed with medical jokes and brief potted biographies of what we had been doing since we last met. I didn't recall Luke taking much part in the conversation. There had to have been more to it than that.

And there was, and when he said I remembered – vaguely, still only vaguely, and with disbelief that something like this could have started under my very nose and I had known nothing about it until a policeman called me in the middle of one night from a place I'd never heard of with the news that Luke Shaw was dead.

Julian Barnes remembered the exact words with which he betrayed himself; well, I suppose he would. I recollected the conversation, but not those vital, deadly words. He had been impressing us, working on his image: I had his medical achievements drawn flirtatiously before me, as a matador flaunts his cape before the frustrated bull, and when he discovered Luke's line of business he couldn't resist demonstrating his prowess in that department too. Except that he got something wrong. Minutely wrong, but fundamentally so: a tiny flaw that must prove fatal to the project he was so proud of.

It could have been a slip of the tongue. We had all been drinking – not heavily but probably enough, especially for Julian who was alone in somebody else's city, tempted by a pleasant chance encounter into being less cautious than he might have been in his own. And he was primarily a medical man: he had a technologist to deal with the minutiae of micro-electronics, he might easily have used the wrong word from somebody else's vocabulary without it having any significance. I imagine that occurred to Luke too; but the suspicion that there was more to it than that had clearly lodged in his skin like a barb that wouldn't come free.

Julian explained to me – painstakingly, almost pedantically, as if it mattered to him that I should appreciate how tiny his error was – just where it was that he had gone wrong. It didn't make any more sense to me the second time than the first, but I laid it down in my memory in layers of amber. It was what I had come for, the piece that completed the puzzle, that finished the picture. It was the piece that would bury him.

Until that fortuitous, fatal meeting he had honestly thought that he was on the right lines, that his work would ultimately give him the results he needed. He had believed himself on the brink of success, the artificial implantable kidney within his reach. The fractional error that Luke picked up from a casual conversation before the professionals at the Schaefer Clinic did from their research dashed that hope. The project could not continue in its present form; correcting it meant going back to basics. It meant throwing out the best part of five years' work, and doing it only months before the scrutineers must decide whether his progress to date justified renewing his grant. In all probability it meant the end of the Barnes AIK.

'You know what I'm saying, Clio? Another ten or fifteen or twenty years of cabinet-sized dialysis machines, of people sicker than they need be tied to a routine like a millstone. Another decade or two of renal medicine dictated by the book-keepers, with finance so short that kidney failure is pretty like a death-sentence for the over-50s. Can you imagine how many lives were at stake, Clio? I owed it them – those countless people for whom viable grafts can't be found, who cope badly with conventional dialysis, or don't even rate a place on a dialysis machine because they're too old or their cases are complicated by other bits of their bodies letting them down – to proceed with a project that offered them the alternative of real hope. I had to succeed; whatever the cost.'

A few days after he returned from London, Luke had contacted him. He had been worrying about the inconsistency, trying to see how he might have misinterpreted Julian's remarks, finally concluding that he had not. Somewhat diffidently he telephoned the Schaefer Clinic to warn the medical lion that his electronics expert had dropped him in it. Julian thanked him politely, never for a moment supposing that he might be right. But when he had that aspect of the project double-checked, he was astonished and horrified to find confirmation of Luke's suspicions.

The timing was crucial. With the grant safely landed he could afford to back-track and sort the problem out. It might take a year or so, but he would still have a functioning AIK well within the five-year term of the grant. But if the trust's scrutineers learned he had been working on a false premise and had nothing to show for their last investment but an apology and a promise to do better next time, there wasn't likely to be another five years. He decided to bluff it out until the cash came through. The chance of discovery was remote. Electronics experts of Luke's calibre didn't spring out of the dew, and on the whole they didn't work for medical funding trusts. There was every reason to hope that the flaw which had eluded Barnes and his own technologist would elude the scrutineers too.

He hoped not to hear from Luke again, but his prayers went unanswered. Luke wanted to know if he had isolated the fault: being amiable and co-operative, and nosey, he would doubtless have offered to help in the search. Julian told him he was mistaken: there was no fault. Luke was certain that there was. He strongly advised Julian to keep looking. He called back, several times. He kept on coming.

Though I had no way of knowing exactly how his mind had worked, it was clear that by this time Luke suspected not error but chicanery. He suspected Barnes of gambling with people's hopes and lives for fame and fortune, and if he could have been sure that I wasn't involved he would have gone straight to the General Medical Council. And he would have been alive today.

Julian was still carefully explaining. 'Finally I saw no option but to put my cards on the table. I told him that he was right but that I couldn't act on it right away; I told him that it would be best from everybody's point of view to wait a few months. Perhaps if he'd believed me – But he didn't. He left me no choice, Clio. I had to silence him. I felt wretched about it and wished to God there was some other way, but he'd left me none.'

A tiny tremor shook my body: someone walking over my grave. It was a warning. The pressure was building up inside me, and I just didn't know how much longer I could keep up this guise of clinical interest. I set my jaw and spoke through my teeth. 'How did you get him to Skipley?'

'I told him – ' He stopped abruptly. I could see him thinking, and the mainly cerebral shrug when he decided there was nothing to gain by lying. 'I told him I would bring you to meet him there, that you would explain the importance of what I was doing, that once he'd heard you out he must do as he thought best.' He eyed me candidly, maybe even a little humour in his gaze, daring me to resent his use of my name more than his murder of my friend.

Even knowing the satisfaction it would give him, I could not but yield to the slow rage mounting through me. I had screwed the lid down pretty tight to manage the interview at all, but this was too much – too bad, worse than I had feared. The fury began behind my knees and surged up the main veins into my heart. It flushed my face and thickened my voice to a barely articulate croak. 'You bastard. You told him *that*?'

'I knew what was holding him back – by then, the only thing. Any time he'd have faced you with it and the last restraint would have been gone. I couldn't buy him, I couldn't bully him, and soon I'd have no rein on his emotions either. I sent him a telegram in your name, booked him into a Skipley boarding house and – well, you know the rest. If it's any comfort, we tried not to hurt him.'

From aching with tension my jaw suddenly went slack and dropped at the sheer effrontery of the man. Not hurt him? They had filled his brain and his eyes with panic, his lungs with dust and no air, and they'd sliced into his wrists with a razor blade. They had held him, watching critically, while his life ebbed out on the carpet, and when it had ended too soon the cynical bastards had brought him back for a bit more. And they'd done it in my name. They couldn't have hurt him more with a welding iron and a circular saw.

Julian had risen behind his half-acre desk. He came round and sat on the arm of my chair and laid his arm across my shoulders in an avuncular embrace. 'I realise how un-pleasant this has all been for you. I wish I could have spared you. When you get your breath back, you'll see I did the only thing possible. I don't expect you to like me for it – '

I leaned forward so that his arm slid down the back of the chair. He straightened up, frowning, but did not try to

83

replace it. He was still close enough to set my skin crawling. I said leadenly, 'What about the boy?'

'The boy?'

'The dead boy in Luke's room.' Dear God: he'd forgotten.

'Oh yes. I don't know who he was. We picked him up off a demolition site and gave him some heroin to play with. He'd have been dead soon anyway.'

I rose – jerkily, like a puppet. I went to the door. With my hand on the gleaming knob I stopped and looked back at him. He was still impressive; with what I knew about him, chillingly so. He was a renaissance man, a brilliant sport in a humdrum world, and there was a terrible temptation – no less compelling for its utter immorality – to think that someone with that intellect and that skill and that boundless potential was entitled to carve his own way free of the endless restrictions that society imposes on smaller souls. The power was on him. He looked as if no one could stand against him.

I said, 'Julian.'

'Yes, Clio.'

'Suffering humanity can't afford the luxury of depending for redemption on a callous megalomaniac like you. I'm going to destroy you; even if the only way is by making you destroy me.'

I walked unhindered out of his door and through the bronze glass tables and potted ferns of the reception area, and across the rose-tinted tarmac to my car. I was back on the motorway before I realised I was shaking.

TWO

I was heading back to Skipley with no clear idea of what to do next. Julian Barnes' candour – though it was what I had gone hoping for – had knocked the wind out of my lungs. He had explained so carefully, so patiently, I had to fight against the cancerous notion that there was after all a kind of harsh sense in what he'd done, that perhaps enough lives could justify – I didn't accept that, of course, couldn't, didn't dare to, because if you accepted that what would follow automatically would rip the foundations out from under what we cherish as civilisation and reduce it to the chaos of a new barbarism. But that he could make me even wonder was a shocking blow to my confidence.

Things look so clear from a distance – deceptively clear and simple. With all I knew it was inconceivable that Barnes could remain at liberty, working on his brilliant, bloody project as if nothing had happened, longer than it would take me to drive to the police station in Skipley. And yet, with all I knew, my ability to prove my allegations was little if at all enhanced by the afternoon's disclosures. Julian was a clever, important, internationally respected man, a man of the highest reputation. I was a former colleague and former lover who had given up medicine to write murder mysteries and wasn't even particularly successful at that. I would tell the police that he had killed Luke rather than have an error in his research made public; he would smile gravely, say that I was clearly disturbed by my traumatic bereavement and recommend the name of a good psychiatrist. I would tell them everything he had told me. He would say, sadly, that it was all fabrication – though I might genuinely believe it – designed to repay him for an old slight, except for the bit about his research. He would say he had indeed made an unfortunate mistake, which he had told me about when I went to see him. The purpose of my visit, he would say, was to try and fan an old ember back to flame; he had bought me lunch and explained gently that he was not interested; I had begun pestering him at his clinic, and finally gone to the police with ludicrous allegations against him. If I was very lucky I might get off with a severe reprimand: a man of Julian's humanity and reputation wouldn't want to bring charges.

He might lose his grant. Or he might not: if he went to the scrutineers immediately, before they heard of his problems from some other source, and told them that he had just discovered a flaw in his research but he knew what to do about it, they might be so impressed by his integrity as to sanction the grant anyway. Even if they didn't – even if they were sufficiently unimpressed as to go through his records again, with a fine-tooth comb, and found that he had to some extent deceived them – it hardly amounted to a criminal offence. Attempting to obtain money by deception? – well, maybe, if the fund was willing to have its business bandied through the courts. Whatever the outcome, it was chicken-feed. He had murdered two people. I didn't want him to walk away with a fine.

But the thing was almost out of my hands. I no longer had options. It did not matter that I thought Chief Inspector Marsh a fool and knew he thought me hysterical; it did not matter that I knew just how fruitful a further interview with him would be. I had been raised in the ethos of law and order and the obligations of citizenship, and still held them in more regard than I might openly have admitted. I had information about a serious crime: whether or not they acted on it was up to them, but I could no longer escape the fact that my duty was to tell the police.

I should have gone straight to the police station when I got back into Skipley. It was almost on my way home, and God knows I'd written often enough about the dire results of putting off till tomorrow revelations about people who'd be glad to see you dead today. But I convinced myself that I'd make a better showing if I washed my face first and took ten minutes with a pencil and the back of an envelope to get my thoughts in order; and I thought maybe I should let Ben know what I was doing too.

There was no need. Charlie Brown was on the phone as I went through the hall and when he saw me he held it out. 'For you.' Ben was calling from the hospital, wondering how I had got on; wondering too, I think, if he should bring round a bucket for the pieces. I waited, pointedly, until Charlie disappeared downstairs and the sound of his door closing came reproachfully to my ears.

Without going into too much detail on an open line I brought Ben up to date. 'I saw him. He admitted it. No, not so much admitted as confirmed. He seemed to think that on the whole it was an act of overwhelming humanity. I told him I'd break him. I'm going to the police now. I expect they'll look at me as if I've crawled out from under a stone and start searching for the Derris, but I don't know what else I can do.'

For a moment he was silent. Then: 'Oh Clio,' he sighed; and then, 'Oh damn. Listen, I'm being paged. Don't go away, I'll get back to you.'

Whatever the emergency was – emergency? Do they have emergencies in a morgue? – it did not detain him long; and it didn't occupy all his attention because when he called me back it was obvious he had been thinking. 'Clio, I've been thinking,' he said. 'I know I made light of it when you were

87

worried, but things have moved on rather since then and I'm not happy that you're safe there any more. I think you should move out.'

'What, right now?' His change of heart was, in all the circumstances, understandable. What it was not was re-assuring.

'As soon as you can,' he urged. 'As soon as you've seen the police. Go back to London, or if you want to stay on here we'll find you somewhere else. But get out of that house tonight.' His voice over the wire was rising, becoming strident.

'Ben – Ben, slow down. I can't just cut and run. I need time – '

'You need ten minutes to pack, that's all,' he insisted. 'Please, Clio, I'm worried about you – no, not worried, I'm scared half to death. You must leave that house. They know it, they know you're there, we know they can walk in any time. Listen. Find the landlord and tell him you're leaving, right now. Then pack your things and pick me up at the hospial, and I'll come to the police with you. Then we'll find somewhere for you to stay tonight and decide what to do tomorrow. Promise me, Clio.'

So I promised him. I was glad to: glad he cared, glad to have the choice made for me, glad I wouldn't have to see Marsh alone, deeply glad to be leaving the genteel dreadful room with its bamboo and brass and the terrible echo of my dead friend's last doglike whimper. I had come to the house to do a job: now I had done it there was not only no good reason for me to stay, there was every reason for me to go. I told Mr Pinner there was nothing more I could do in his house and was deliberately vague about where I was going. Polite as ever, he was patently as glad to see me leaving as I was to go.

As I went into my flat, closing the door behind me, the radio came on, loudly.

The next I remember clearly was watching a man arranging strange objects on my table. I didn't know what it meant, except that it meant I was in trouble. I was propped, some-what groggily, in a fireside chair and held there by two pairs of nylon tights – one an everyday pair but one my best Saturday night lurex – binding my wrists to the wooden arms. My eyes weren't focusing properly and my face felt stiff: the latter effect was due to a broad strip of surgical tape across my mouth, the former something to do with the few minutes that had gone missing between opening the door and watching my table fill up with unconnected, strangely ominous objects like a test of memory.

There was my typewriter, that I had hardly used since I arrived here but could no more have left behind than my toothbrush. There was a small pile of blank paper and a pen. There was a hypodermic syringe and a small glass bottle, almost full. There was a bottle of household bleach.

The radio was down to normal volume: enough to cover the sound of low voices, too quiet to provoke complaints – or memories.

There were two of them: two big, strong young men, one of them very big indeed. They were the boob enhancer and the jogger's ankle expert from the Schaefer Clinic. Without their white coats they looked even less like real doctors; but right enough, when he spoke, the bigger of them – Chandos – rounded his vowels as though his life, or at least his accep-tance at the hunt ball, depended on it.

'Feeling better, Dr Rees? Oh good. Sorry about that: a necessary precaution, I'm sure you understand.'

Too true I understood. Before I knew which way was up I understood.

Chandos was the kindest thing that could have happened to Harwich. By contrast he looked almost a normal size; he also spoke like a normal person instead of neighing like a horse. He looked up briefly from the table, where he was filling the syringe. 'Save your breath. She's not interested in your bedside manner.' His accent was lightly burred, an upper-crust variant on the speech of the Peaks, and there was no mistaking the stab of intelligence in the glance of his steel grey eyes. His nose had been broken at some time and there was a network of old scars grained into one cheek: souvenirs of either a small war or a rugby friendly.

Two of them: where was Barnes? I couldn't ask but I could move my head enough to squint over both shoulders. The back of my neck protested as only a hurt neck can, but I persisted until I was sure he wasn't waiting behind me.

Harwich read my eyes. 'He didn't come.'

If there had been any room for doubt about their intentions, that removed it. To frighten me, to bully me, even to knock some sense into me, he'd have come. He had stayed away because he didn't want to watch me die. I nodded, feeling my body respond with a slow, profound lurch like the start of an avalanche, as if all my insides were starting to dissolve. I felt them turn and slump, squeezed to soup by gut muscles that thought – like many a nanny – that bowel evacuation was the answer to all human ills. Then I drove both heels into the mock-Turkey carpet with all the force I could muster and the chair crashed over backwards on to the floor that was also Charlie's ceiling.

It was an act of sheer desperation. I didn't know if he was down there still. I still didn't know if he was involved in this, and if not what quality of help I could expect from him – even if he didn't merely shrug off the racket as more eccentric behaviour from the loonie upstairs. It was a long shot. It was the only shot I could play, and I wouldn't get playing it twice.

The shattering impact raced through my spine from coccyx to cerebellum, an explosive shock to a body which hadn't yet got over being mugged, and between pain and nausea I thought for several moments that I was going to faint. I·fought back the surging grey, because I knew there wouldn't be many chances of getting out of this and I didn't want to miss one, and gradually the cloying tide withdrew and I could see again.

My visitors had frozen at the sudden cacophony. Now their blood and minds were moving again. Harwich started to the door and listened at the keyhole; after a space of silence he opened it a crack and looked and listened again. Then he closed it, apparently satisfied. Oh well. Chandos loomed over me like an impending thunderstorm. I winked at him, partly for the good of my battered ego but mostly to see if his apoplexy was as imminent as it promised, and he shoved out hands like refugees from a butcher's shop. I flinched automatically but the mayhem stopped at his eyes. He was only lifting the chair.

As my weight shifted forward pain stabbed and I yelled into my gag. I thought my arm was broken. But there was no crepitus and no visible distortion, so I told myself maybe it was just bruised in the fall, and only then did it strike me that it probably didn't matter a damn. It hurt, but the fear hurt more.

Harwich came back from the door. He wasn't approaching apoplexy. He wasn't even angry. The slow gaze he laid on me was wary, appraising, shot through with a respect that was neither grudging nor compassionate. Certain ancient warriors would spare a vanquished enemy who showed particular courage: that was the way he was looking at me. Not that he was contemplating a similar generosity – he couldn't afford to, he had to do what he'd come here for – but when it was done he wouldn't quickly bury me with the rest of his mistakes under the trees at the back of his mind. He would remember that gesture of defiance a long time. It was something; but it wasn't much.

He came forward, skirting the table without sparing it a glance, and perched himself on the edge. 'You know why we're here, of course.' I nodded again, mute. 'Of course you do. We're going to kill you. But first we want something from you. A suicide note.'

You can't laugh with surgical tape across your mouth. I'm not sure I could have done anyway, but I made a brave attempt at muffled derision, deriving a certain wan comfort from the thought that if he couldn't hear me laugh he couldn't hear me sob either.

He got the point. He did not smile. 'I know, you think I'm crazy. I'm not. We've given it a lot of thought, and when you have too you'll do as we ask.' He spread a hand towards the collection on the table behind him. 'For a start, think about this lot.'

I did, and I did not like the answers I was coming up with. He saw that too, the perceptive bastard.

'That's right. We have here the props for two scenarios. The first is where you decide to be sensible. You take the pen and paper and write out the kind of note policemen expect to find near suicides. The kind of note Chief Inspector Marsh will believe was written by a woman who, deranged by the death of a close friend, holds her own profession guilty of murder and the police of failing to solve it. So she launches on a crazy crusade to bring the killer to justice, and when she's faced with her own inevitable failure she tells her landlord she's leaving and takes her own life with a massive overdose of diamorphine – stolen, and reported stolen, from the Schaefer Clinic at a time roughly concurrent with your visit.' That accounted for the pen, the paper, the syringe and the little glass bottle.

The typewriter? The bleach? 'The second is where you let your righteous indignation get in the way of your common sense. In that eventuality you type out your suicide note and kill yourself by downing a bottle of bleach. It's the one from under your sink: any fingerprints on it will be yours or Shaw's – I of course am wearing gloves.' He was, too –

surgeon's gloves, the ultimate protection against washday hands.

There was no need to spell it out further. The syringe contained a lethal dose of bliss, the plastic bottle a slow death of appalling agony. Either way my end was assured; either way my suicide note would be believed. It would explain away the more bizarre side-issues to Luke's death. My allegations discredited, my motives understood, his murder would be reinstated as just another sordid little slaying of a homosexual. Marsh would be happy to have it so: he would understand that much better than the curious postulations I had wished on him. Only Ben might protest the absurdity of my suicide, as I had protested Luke's; but he had no more proof than I had, and I thought him less obdurate. He would sorrow for me but he would not avenge me or even die trying. No one would. Julian Barnes and his lieutenants would escape scot-free the consequences of three murders and a daring fraud.

I thought about it, but I didn't think about it long. It was no contest. I didn't want to die: more, I didn't want to be killed by these medical abortions. But most of all I didn't want to die of a pint of powerful corrosive down my oesophagus. I'd had to deal with such cases in casualty at my hospital. You could hear them coming from the main gate. I didn't want to go that way. Anything was preferable, including writing their goddamned little note. It wouldn't make any difference, except to me. It was only Julian Barnes' famous perfectionism that insisted on a hand-written note. Marsh would think nothing odd of an author tapping out her last words on her trusty portable.

'Well,' said Harwich from the table. 'Which is it to be?'

'Heaven or hell?' added Chandos, an obscene leer in his voice, an unhealthy flush still on his long cheeks that hovered above me like a gibbous moon. He was staying behind the chair to forestall a repeat performance.

I exercised my eybrows in a kind of facial shrug. It was the only form of expression left to me if the silly sods wouldn't present me with a yes-or-no question.

Harwich at least understood the problem. 'Will you co-operate?' he asked in a low, clear voice while a strange mist of an expression veiled across his face. Incredibly, I recognised it as humiliation. It was as if his small, stupid, inconsequential error had fractured the shell of infallibility which protected him from a confrontation with what he was doing. He did – they both did – what Barnes told him, and he did it unquestioningly because Barnes was an Olympian, a kind of demigod who twisted the world to his needs rather than the other way round. He believed that particularity, that almost messianic quality, extended to himself by association and that he could do no wrong while he did the master's work. His tiny, idiotic slip, and my apprehension of it, spoiled that for him. For a moment the sense of being special, chosen, failed him and the image of himself as a common murderer came flooding in. He didn't like that, not a bit, but his surge of resentment was directed not at Julian but at me, so it didn't promise to do me much good. I nodded a third time.

'Good girl,' neighed the moon above me. He had curly fair hair and a tie I'm sure I was supposed to recognise. I stared up his nose, hating him – not only for what he was doing but for treating me like a bit of fluff when I'd qualified while he was still trying to work out whether his mouth or his ear was the right place for a spoonful of porridge.

Harwich only nodded back at me, a slow burning in his eyes like embers.

They hefted the chair over to the table and freed my right arm. I took the proffered pen. I stared at the paper. It stared back at me, blank and empty as the oblivion it represented.

'Write.'

I wrote: 'It is a far, far better thing that I do now – '

I don't think Chandos recognised it. Harwich snatched

away the top sheet with an angry gesture and crumpled it into his pocket. 'I'll tell you what to write.' He had brought a sample suicide note with him, and he began dictating at a measured pace.

It was good stuff, full of remorse and grief and the muted torment of the arguably insane. When they read that at the inquest there wouldn't be a dry eye in the house. It said a lot of things, but mostly what it said was that neither Julian Barnes nor anyone else at the Schaefer Clinic was involved in either Luke's death or my own.

Harwich sounded, and knew he sounded, pretty damn silly reading this purple prose aloud, particularly at half speed, and when he realised I wasn't taking it down he felt sillier still. He ground to a halt, glaring at me with deep dislike, and his spare hand strayed over the table to the bleach. But then the anger leached out of his eyes and confusion strayed in, because the funny shape my face had gone was the result of trying to grin through a mask of surgical tape. '*Now* what?' he whispered, and his voice held a note of despair.

My eyes beamed at him and I shook my head. It wasn't that funny, the bottom line was still me pushing up daisies, but the worst threat was meaningless. The relief was such that I felt positively light-headed with it. When you've contemplated death by calcium oxychloride, the promise of death by diamorphine is like winning the pools.

I wrote: 'You can't use the bleach, whatever I write or don't write. If Barnes reported the diamorphine stolen, it has to be found here or the police will continue investigating. And if it's here, nobody will believe that I used any other means of suicide.' I scrawled as a post-script, 'You blew it.'

You can't imagine how good his expression made me feel. When they found me on the floor, the happy smile on my face would not be due to diamorphine alone.

'She's right,' ground Harwich, 'the cow.'

95

'I don't understand,' Chandos complained.

'No.' Harwich folded his speech back into his pocket. He picked up the syringe, automatically fountaining the contents although an air embolism was the least of my worries now. His voice was bleak. 'Hold her.'

'Julian said – '

'Hold her, damn you.'

The angle you inject yourself from is different from that at which you inject someone else: at least they thought of that. They closed round me, a ring of muscle and good tweed that seemed composed of much more than just two young men. I struggled, I kicked; I landed a satisfyingly substantial swing in a groin like Cardigan Bay and only wished I'd been wearing stilettos instead of mocassins; hands like mechanical grabs locked my body to the chair. With nothing else left to me, I screamed silently into my gag and watched the needle line up on my vein.

Behind Harwich's left shoulder the door exploded inward with a crack like gunfire. I had a brief, fragmentary impression of a baseball boot being followed into the room, very fast, by a string-thin body, a flaxen head and a couple of six-guns, and then a voice I scarcely recognised, hard and deadly, bit out the words, 'Back away from her, slowly.'

THREE

It was Charlie. The baseball boots, the whip-thin body, the mane of yellow hair, even the savage gravelly voice, were all Charlie, but the six-guns were an illusion. He held in his right hand an aerosol can and in his left a long-nosed gas stove lighter, and from the way he held them he clearly considered the combination lethal.

The two men wrapped around my torso apparently thought so too, or at least weren't prepared to call the bluff. First they froze, the immobile weight of them on my chest suffocating. Then they straightened up, slowly and awkwardly, unfolding to either side of the chair, their eyes on Charlie and his improbable weaponry. He came forward from the door and they stepped back. 'So wise,' he murmured, his voice·thick with a bridled fury that burbled in his throat like blood.

With the undefined menace of can and lighter he drove them back across the room, only stopping when his long leg, his ancient denims the colour of a January sky over Morecambe, brushed against my hand. He glanced down briefly, and with the lighter drew a line of heat along the side of the wooden arm which parted my best Saturday lurex in a fused and smelly hank that dripped a couple of hot spots on my skin as I pulled my wrist free.

'You all right?'

My hands were shaking so much that I couldn't find the

97

edge of the surgical tape. I nodded vigorously.

'Go outside and start your car. I'll be out in a minute.'

I didn't like leaving him with them. Weight for weight he was outnumbered three to one. But he seemed in control of the situation, and I could see the urgent desirability of a car sitting outside with the engine running. I scanned the room for my bag. It was by the door, where I must have dropped it. I snatched it up, fished out the keys and scuttled across the hall and down the front steps. The Citroen, bless its little sewing machine of a heart, started first turn; I revved the engine so Charlie would hear it and waited, my eyes flicking anxiously between the front door and my window. I finally got a fingernail under the tape and ripped it off.

Unwanted hair? Forget wax, razors, creams and expensive electrolysis – surgical tape is the answer every time.

Suddenly Charlie was out of the door and bounding the steps four at a time. He'd lost the aerosol but was still brandishing the lighter. Springing past the only other car drawn up outside the house he swung the heavy object by its long snout and crashed it through the windscreen. It was a pity, really, because it was Mr Pinner's sister's car – the hoodlums from the clinic must have parked round the corner. Charlie flung himself into the Citroen and I sped off, racing up through a gearbox that is not so much individual as hand-knitted. There was no pursuit.

I don't know what bit of me was doing the driving – some bit that had somehow managed to miss the events of the last half-hour, I think, because it was not only calmer and better controlled than the rest of me but it had also managed to hang on to some of its wits. It drove to the busiest part of Skipley – the car park in front of the railway station – and parked there in full view of five bored taxi drivers, the crew and passengers of two buses and anything up to a hundred assorted persons meeting or being met from trains. I can't say I felt safe there – I doubted if I'd ever feel safe again – but

98

it was an antidote of a kind to the awesome sense of loneliness I had experienced in my queer suburban flatlet before Charlie had blazed through the door, a little like a hippy Superman and a little like the Seventh Cavalry.

'Jesus,' Charlie said with quiet reverence, 'imagine making a get-away in a 2CV!'

It had been done before, of course, but I didn't feel up to telling him by whom. I didn't say anything. At first I thought it was because I didn't want to; then I realised I couldn't. I felt my respiration increase until I was hyperventilating, and though I knew it I couldn't do anything about it.

Charlie slid a long arm round my shoulders, exerting a gentle pressure on my rigid body. Slowly it yielded to the warmth of him, slumping by degrees against his side. 'Okay, that's good,' he murmured into the top of my head, 'now just relax your jaw so you can yell if you want to.'

I didn't know what I wanted but I did as he said, and when I got my teeth apart the last of the awful tension broke with a gasp and I went as limp as a week-old lettuce.

Charlie got out and came round the car, and gently shunted me over into the passenger seat. 'Nothing personal,' he said, 'but three red lights is enough for one evening. Clio, you want to tell me what happened in there?'

I told him: what, and why, and who. When I had finished I had a question of my own. 'What did you do to them?'

'*Do* to them? Do me a favour.' His voice ran up with indignation and awe. 'Did you see the *size* of those guys? I sprayed Damp Start in their faces and ran like hell.'

We sat a minute longer, recovering. Then Charlie started the engine. 'Time we brought the police up to date.'

'Oh God,' I moaned, 'not again.'

'I know. But this time you have a witness.'

'You'd think it would be enough, wouldn't you?' I agreed lugubriously. 'But you don't know the lad who's dealing with it. He makes Mr Plod look like Fabian of the Yard. He'll probably decide I put you up to it.'

Something peculiar was happening to Charlie's narrow face: a twitchy sort of something that could have been the start of a particularly nasty disease of the nervous system, although in other circumstances you'd have sworn he was trying not to laugh. Emotions I could not identify burred in his voice. 'Clio, I have a confession. I was put up to it. What's more, Harry Marsh knows it. Harry Marsh did it.'

It all came out as he was driving, punctuated by gear-changes like a swampie wrestling an alligator. He was not a cello student, although he pointed out with obvious pride that he was no mean cellist, but a security consultant. He had done a diploma course in it, at which many of the lecturers were retired criminals, but what with the recession and firms having little worth protecting beside their overdraft statements, business had been decidedly quiet and when Chief Inspector Marsh called up an old favour and asked him to turn watch-dog for a week or so there had been no good reason to refuse.

The policeman had believed what I'd told him – all of it, right from the start – and when he had expressed concern for my safety he had been absolutely serious. But I hadn't asked for protection, had given him no reason to suppose I would accept or co-operate with a formal guardian, and in any event the evidence, as distinct from his instincts, hardly justified the expenditure of police time in a long, trying and quite possibly unnecessary surveillance operation. So he'd asked Charlie to keep an eye on me, off the record.

'Harry and me, we go way back,' he declared expansively, but it couldn't have been that far back because Marsh would have been collecting his twenty-year medal about the time Charlie received his diploma. 'I owed him one. It seemed no big thing when he called me – I didn't know I'd end up grappling with the medical mafia.'

I tried to smile at him but it was too soon. It was still all too real. A shudder ran the length of me. 'Did I remember to say thank you?'

He grinned at me, boyishly. 'I forget.' He was over it already. Fifteen minutes before he had looked and sounded, and so far as I could judge had been, ready to use his ad-lib weaponry to maim or kill. But that time was already past, leaving no shadows. He wouldn't wake screaming from dreams in which he took a minute longer to find the cold-start spray and the gas gun, or couldn't kick the door in. I was glad for him. With the unpretentious efficiency of his generation he had identified the problem, improvised a means of dealing with it, and put the whole nasty episode behind him as soon as it was safe to do so. It was an admirable philosophy, a splendid way to be: confident in the strength and invulnerability of his youth. I envied him, but most of all I wondered at my own lack of perspicacity. While I had been right to doubt his bona fides, I must have viewed him with a very jaundiced eye to suspect Charlie of malice. It's not for me to say there are no more honest or open faces than his, only that they usually come with wings, a halo and a harp.

I whistled, slowly and shakily. 'Charlie Brown, I've been a bloody fool. It nearly cost me my life. But for you it would have done. If there's ever anything I can do in return – tonsillectomy, appendicectomy, prostate, piles – '

He laughed, shaking his head, and I laughed too, and then I saw we were running out of road. 'Charlie!'

The police station was offset from the centre of the town, a newish building that had been the first stage in redeveloping the decayed inner ring between the busy trading heart and the prosperous commercial outskirts. The main phase of work was now commencing in surrounding back-streets, and there were signs posted to the lamp-standards apologising for the unavoidable inconvenience. The road was up.

It had come up since the last time I was this way, with Ben, but with heavy plant I don't suppose it takes long to carve a trench three feet wide and deep enough that the sides disappeared into the darkness. It stretched from the wall of the premises on one side of the road into the middle on the building site on the other, and they had thoughtfully provided a boardwalk bridge for the benefit of pedestrians.

The Citroen's hydraulic brakes hauled us up with the V-shaped bumper practically under the red-and-white barrier plank. We sat for a moment gazing at the artist's impression of what the finished job would look like. 'What, no casino?' said Charlie.

'Where do we go from here?'

Out-of-towners both, we neither of us knew the intimate back alleys that networked Skipley like a hundred other essentially Victorian towns. There would be a way round, of course, but none was immediately apparent. We could spend a long time looking.

'Back to the ring road,' decided Charlie, 'and in from the other side.'

He swung the Citroen through a three-point-turn and pointed her back towards the suburbs. His mastery of the gear-change was growing: less like wrestling an alligator, more like strangling a chicken. By mutual if unvoiced consent we put in a broad dogleg to avoid the immediate vicinity of the Indian Mutiny.

Even so, I caught him paying close attention to the rear view mirror and realised with a small sick shock that he'd gone suddenly quiet, watchful and deliberate. He said soberly, 'Do you know anyone with a brown Cortina?'

I screwed round in my seat but saw nothing to either alarm or reassure me. The long day – dear God, was it only this afternoon I burst into Julian Barnes' office? – was finally drawing in and the gathering dusk prevented me from seeing into the dim car. Like ourselves it was riding on sidelights, a dark bulk ghosting along behind us like a shadow. It could have been anyone. I tried to cast my mind back to the clinic car-park but all I could remember was the gate I'd been so glad to get behind me. I had thought I was safe then. It hadn't occurred to me that the one place he couldn't afford to bloody was his own doorstep.

I said edgily, 'I don't know what they were driving.'

Other vehicles joined us in the exodus. With cross-town access severely limited, it was inevitable that pressure on these spoke-routes feeding the ring road would be increased. 'It's probably just coincidence,' said Charlie, but he kept one eye on the mirror as he drove.

The traffic flowing along the ring road was bright and busy and copious, a promise of protection from the menace that grew in darkness and isolation. I felt the hearts of both of us lighten as we joined it. The Cortina, now three or four cars back, turned the other way.

'What did I tell you?' said Charlie cheerfully, thinking I wouldn't hear the note of relief in his voice. 'Coincidence. Now, how do we get at Harry's nicking shop?'

The ring road was a wheel supported by ten or a dozen spokes radiating from the town centre. Perhaps half of them continued out behind the by-pass, feeding the industrial estates, a handful of large housing developments, the motorway to the north-east and several lesser arterials into the surrounding country, which like Skipley itself was insufficiently interesting to tempt the traveller out of his way. Skipley was a place for working in, for making money in, and for performing those messy little murders that nobody wants too close to home.

We let a couple of junctions go by, then Charlie moved the Citroen — did I tell you it was yellow? No. You guessed, though, didn't you? — into the outside lane ready to make a right turn at the third. Fifty yards ahead the traffic lights changed up and Charlie changed down, and we rolled to a halt at the head of a small cortege of inbound vehicles in the sliproad.

'Can you find your way from here?'

'If I can't I'll find a phone box and let them come and get us.'

The inside lane filled quickly, the outside lane – the one beside us – more slowly. Looking across the junction we saw the same thing happening with the on-coming traffic, except that there wasn't a road beyond the ring road so there was no sliproad. The outer lane filled slower than ours, led by one of those drivers who'll do anything – creep, cruise in neutral, ride his clutch or throw out a couple of drag 'chutes – rather than actually stop at traffic lights. He probably worked it out once on his pocket calculator that stopping cost him a penny-farthing in petrol.

Traffic coming out of town turned across our bows heading north, or else south along the dual carriageway, back towards Pinner's Raj. The lights changed again. The Citroen began her turn.

Sudden movement where none should have been drew our eyes like a shriek. Horns blared. The car opposite, that hadn't stopped, was coming like a train, all the power of his big engine behind him, with a disregard for the red light facing him as deliberate as it was total.

There was a long moment you would not expect there to be: long enough for conversation, of a kind.

'Christ, Charlie!'

'How'd they get there?' hissed Charlie in his teeth.

The answer, of course, was by knowing their way round this town a damn sight better than we did, but now was not the time to be worrying about it. The only point of immediate relevance was that an accelerating Cortina would roll over the top of the 2CV6 without losing much more than paint and a couple of miles an hour. They would be twenty miles away before anyone started looking, and we would be toothpaste.

Charlie wrenched the wheel back with all the strength in his narrow shoulders. I don't know if he had reasoned it out, if he was acting on instinct or simply from panic and the need to do something. There wasn't enough acceleration in the dinky two-horse engine to carry us out of the path of the tank bearing down on us, and by trying he would have exposed our vulnerable flank: instead he met her head on, with the solidest part of our structure between our frail bodies and a hurtling ton of brown steel.

How we should have fared in a head-on collision I prefer not to speculate. We might have survived with only shattered legs, perhaps an amputation or two. Surprised by Charlie's unorthodox manoeuvre the driver – I think it was Harwich: a fraction more light was passing through the saloon on the driver's side than on the passenger's – hesitated, and in the instant's grace that won us Charlie had the yellow eggshell back across the destroyer's bows and a sliver of a chance was opening before us.

Horns again and the squeal of brakes as the north-bound traffic which had moved off when we did tried to make a space for us. There was a savage jolt as the Citroen bucketed on to the central reservation like a hunter tackling an Irish bank, and then the monstrous bludgeoning impact that Charlie's best efforts could not finally protect us from. I crashed into my seat-belt as if fired from a gun; rather numbly I supposed this was the end.

Somehow the Citroen kept her feet. The outer end of the Cortina's bumper slammed into her just forward of the rear wheel and the collision flung her bodily into the north-bound carriageway. Under the contradictory sway of powerful forces she teetered wildly on various combinations of two wheels before finally grounding, bouncing once and yielding to something like control. Charlie saw a gap in the traffic and took it, accelerating away from the shocked and angry confusion of the violated junction.

Only then did the full magnitude of our escape strike me. We should have been dead – or worse, a bloody pulp of horrific injuries still containing a spark or two of life in a smouldering tangle of twisted metal. Instead we were not only alive but uninjured; the car was largely intact, certainly still viable; our assailants were already out of sight astern; and we were still travelling, widening the distance between us with every passing second, and not about to stop for anything.

FOUR

'No way,' said Charlie, with conviction, shaking his yellow head. In the backwash of street-lights and headlamps his face was ashen, drawn by vertical lines as deeply graven as scars. The greyness was in his voice too. The events of the evening had finally got to him, ageing him ten years. He sounded sick. Before today he hadn't really believed that people went around murdering one another – knew it, perhaps, from reading the newspapers, but never really believed. What the hell, a month ago I hadn't believed it either. 'I'm not going back in there. Those bloody back-streets: sooner or later we'd hit another dead end and those bastards would be waiting for us.'

The crash had shaken him badly – more than me, perhaps shaving death can become a habit like anything else, given the chance, and familiarity begins to breed complacency if not contempt – and his nerve had broken. He had seen death under the grill of the car thundering at him and he would never believe himself invulnerable again. That phase of his youth was past.

I tried not to argue with him, to give him the chance to heal. I felt a responsibility for him, because saving my life had cost him something that could never be restored. 'We must contact the police.'

'Yes.' He was driving hunched over the wheel, awkward and defensive in the unreasonable length of him, checking the road behind obsessively in snatched glances. 'Yeah. Well, like I say, they can come to us. Lights – that's what we need, bright lights. The motorway. We'll get on to the motorway and call from one of the service stations. That way we'll see if there's anyone after us, and they can only come one way.'

'Charlie.' I laid my hand on his arm where his shirt sleeve was turned back and felt the nerves leap beneath the skin. 'Calm down. You've done a good job. You've pulled my chestnuts out of the fire not once but twice. Harry Marsh will be proud of you. I'm proud of you. I know you feel awful now. It's shock, it'll pass. Tonight we'll drink ourselves into a maudlin stupor and hold hands and cry, and tomorrow we'll be fine. And it'll all be over.'

He sucked in a deep breath and after a moment his head rocked back. I could feel the tension beginning to ease in his long muscles. The plane of his white cheek turned a fraction towards me, reflecting the rhythmic pulses of the passing lights, and he forced a twitchy grin. 'Yeah. Sorry.'

I shook my head. 'Thanks.'

The motorway sprang out of the gathering dark like a river of fairy-lights in the dip, towards which the ring road bore its voyager-captives like a fairground ride. At the last moment, when it seemed about to plunge us into that torrent of brilliant traffic, the dual carriageway picked itself up and hurled itself over a bridge, the cataract of lights and the curious, unmistakable motorway rumble disappearing beneath us. We took the sliproad after the bridge that brought us down to join the convoy of cars and lumbering lorries heading south-east. We went that way because north-west the motorway went to Birmingham.

Ten miles down the road, with Charlie beginning to look himself again, his natural buoyancy reasserting itself with every unmolested minute that passed, the blue and white signs gave warning of services ahead. A village of lights leapt up like an oasis on the left.

Charlie had been dwelling on the mirror for the last couple of miles. Chewing on his cheek he said, 'Well, I can't see anything. Let's give it a swing.' He signalled at the last possible moment and veered off into the deceleration lane. No one followed.

We parked carefully, as close as we could get to the telephone in the main hall of the building while still out of sight of traffic coming off the motorway. There was nothing we could do about the height or banana-yellowness of the Citroen, but by placing her judiciously between the back wall of the public conveniences and a rubbish skip we made her as unobtrusive as we could. A driver cruising quickly through the parking zone would not have spotted her.

Charlie went to the phone. I positioned myself on a dark corner from where I could watch both the car and the bright glass arcade. Still no one came. The traffic on the motorway was thinning perceptibly and almost none of it was taking advantage of the service station.

It wasn't five minutes before Charlie was back, walking briskly, even a little jauntily. 'I talked to Harry. I told him what happened. He's sending a car for us. It'll be here in half an hour. Do you fancy a coffee while we wait?'

Fancy wasn't the word. I craved coffee as pregnant women crave cabbage and ice-cream, as small men with big noses and ulcers crave power, but just then I remembered something even more pressing. 'Ben! I was supposed to pick him up at the hospital. He was worried before – he'll be climbing the walls by now. I'll have to call him, let him know I'm all right.'

'Okay,' said Charlie, 'I'll get the coffee in. Er – can you lend me the money?' He'd had nothing in his pockets when he answered the peremptory summons of my chair hitting the floor. He'd had to reverse the charges to call the police station.

I did not know where I would find Ben. If he had been waiting at the hosptial gates since we last spoke he had probably frozen to a permanent fixture. Or he might have gone home. I tried his hospital extension and he answered the phone on the second ring. I could hear the sweat on his brow.

Charlie had taken a table overlooking the forecourt. The choice was wide, the place almost empty. We broke open a packet of biscuits and munched mechanically, tasting nothing. That could have been the biscuits, of course.

'Did you get him?'

'He'd chewed his fingernails back to the elbow.'

'There's one thing I don't understand about all this,' said Charlie, thoughtfully pouring sugar into his third cup. If the police car took much longer I'd be broke too, except that the cafeteria was closing around us. 'Well, lots of things really, but one thing in particular. Why Skipley? What's so special about hole-in-the-wall bloody Skipley that people travel from miles around to murder and be murdered there?'

I shrugged. 'I don't suppose it had to be Skipley, just that it happened to be. Barnes wouldn't want to foul his own nest, so that ruled out the Birmingham area – Skipley was far enough from the clinic to be safe, near enough to be handy.'

'I guess.' Charlie sounded unconvinced. Then he grinned. 'Harry thinks it's all part of a plot against him.'

Finally taking the hint, we wandered out of the canteen – which closed behind us, with a bang – and through the concourse. The space invader machines were pinging salvos at each other, and a cast-iron elephant lurked dismally in a corner, waiting for the child's coin that would bring him to cheery, if temporary, life. He looked he was in for a long wait. Apart from ourselves the only people on the concourse were three youths in motorcycle leathers, who seemed unlikely to be turned on by a flaking Dumbo. The only remaining activity was over at the petrol pumps, where the first of the night's revellers vied with the last of the homing workers for a vacant hose. It was entirely dark now and the filling station was an island of white light separated from the main building by a dark bight of car-park. The car-park too was all but empty.

As we strolled towards the door, managing with a small effort to stay loose and talk of other things besides the inordinate length of time the police car was taking to get here, the motorcyclists jostled past us, laughing and jeering. 'Nice motor, mate, what did you do – forget to open the garage door?'

I smiled indulgently, thinking that even a 2CV would roll over a motorbike in a quite satisfactory way, and Charlie yelled after them, 'Wait till you lot need something to take the carry-cot and the mother-in-law.'

I grinned at him, then the grin froze over. As casually and firmly as I could I steered Charlie away from the floodlit entrance. Under the pretext of a game of Super Thing (The Ultimate Nightmare: Get The Thing Before The Thing Gets You) I leaned close and hissed at him, 'That's a funny thing to say about a Deux Chevaux with a dent in the side.'

Comprehension, quickly followed by apprehension, washed over his long face. The sea-green eyes he focused on me were sharp. 'You think there's another battered car out there – a big brown one with the bumper bashed in?'

'How do we see if it's them without them – if it's them – seeing us?'

We found a service door at the back and crept along the blank wall to where we had left the Citroen. There was no one near it. Charlie whispered to me to stay with it but I wasn't going to let him go alone, or be left alone come to that. We inched up the darkness behind the skip. The corner of the building gave us an oblique view across the car-park but still no answer: faint glints marked a dozen or so vehicles left on the tarmac but gave no clue as to what they were or whether they were occupied.

Then the motorcycles started up in a roar of pistons and quartered the car-park with scythes of white light and there it was, tucked away near the back, big and brown and grinning savagely with the bright damage to the offside front wing. A figure was momentarily silhouetted behind the wheel.

'Where's the other one?'

'Where's the goddamned blue-and-white?'

Suddenly Charlie had my hand and was running me back towards the Citroen. 'Come on, we're getting out of here.'

'Charlie! What about the police?'

'You think we'll be here to meet them if we hang around much longer?'

I didn't know. I honestly didn't know. Something had gone wrong: a puncture, a breakdown, an accident, something to delay them. There was simply no way to gauge how much longer they might be. Nor could we know what Barnes' cowboys intended now, except that they'd had the chance of a clean escape after the battle of the ring road, and they hadn't thrown it away merely for the opportunity to exchange insurance numbers. By any reasoned assessment it was madness for them still to be pursuing us. They had to be certain in their own minds that the result would be worth the risk. Perhaps Charlie was right. But if we left here there was no knowing when or where we might find help. The one sure thing was that we needed some.

'We can't outrun them in my car.'

'Not on the motorway, no,' he agreed darkly. He released the handbrake and we pushed the Citroen back round the far corner, so that the bulk of the building stood between us and the Cortina and only the perimeter fence lay behind. It was like pushing a pram. We got in and quietly closed the doors. 'There's a map in the cafe. I had a look at it while you were on the phone. On a clear day you can see three castles, two hill-forts and a stone circle.'

It was pitch dark around us. I couldn't see the point. 'So?'

'We're high up. Behind the platform they built this place on the land drops away steeply into a valley, with a few farms linked by little rural roads in the bottom. Down there we could hold our own against a Porsche.'

'Ah.' My new friend Charlie was no mug. He'd found us a fire escape. 'And how do we get down there?'

'Hopefully we find a gap in the fence along here somewhere. Otherwise we make one.'

We found one. A long vehicle had tried turning in a short space and punched the paling out from between two posts. It lay on the steep scree well below the lip and bounced us a foot into the air as we careered down at 30 mph without lights.

'Charlie,' I stammered in time to the jouncing suspension, 'can you actually see where you're steering?'

'You think I'd be doing this if I could see what it was I was doing?'

The Citroen, hurtling headlong into the black, caught something solid with her nearside front wheel and catapulted sideways, ready to turn over with the unexpended momentum. But for the scree sliding away beneath her, giving an outlet for that pent-up velocity, I'd have been claiming the medal or whatever it is Citroen award owners who manage to roll their 2CVs. It would have looked good on my coffin. Somehow, though, the skittering shifting ground, letting her travel sideways down the slope, put off the moment of truth until a combination of good luck and Charlie could bring her nose round and restore some semblance of control.

Charlie said in a tight, thin voice, 'I think maybe you're right,' and switched the headlights on.

The white beam made a tunnel in the night, a sure beacon if anyone missing us was crazy enough to look off the edge of the world. The advantages were meagre by comparison. The terrible beating the car was taking from the steep and stony

113

hill was translated into a wild oscillation of the probing light, up and down and from side to side. Nothing it captured resolved itself sensibly before the spotlight yawed on to something else: all we got were kaleidoscopic impressions such as an avalanche might receive on its roller-coaster progress down a tortured mountain. All the light did was present a visual version of the corruscating chaos that filled our ears and pummelled our bodies. It made nothing easier; rather it expanded the scope for fear.

More like a yachtsman than a driver, Charlie jockeyed the car grimly from crisis to crisis, hanging on to her wavering nose, trying to pick up obstacles while there was still time to avoid them, tentatively dabbing at the brake where the going felt firmest.

We felt rather than saw the slope beginning to run out. The inexorable tow of gravity drew less urgently, the clatter of stones beneath the car grew less deafening and the headlights stopped cartwheeling across half the valley. Charlie played the steering, swinging the beam in a wide swathe before us. Finally he gave a satisfied little grunt and drove right. We moved from scree on to rough grass and stopped at a gate. I was glad about that. Only in Hollywood capers are the gates made of half-inch planking – in the British countryside they are commonly made of tubular steel and angle-iron and fastened with a decade of chain that would fire anything less than a tank back where it came from with the approximate muzzle velocity of a cannon.

After the gate there was a field, and after the next gate there was a lane. The Citroen trundled on to the cracked tarmac with a creaky sigh, like an elderly lady rescued from a skateboard. Unflatteringly underlit by the dashboard backlight, Charlie and I regarded each other speculatively.

'Free and clear?'

'Where have I heard that before?'

'Let's find a telephone.'

114

It was while we were driving down that lane in search of a farmhouse that I began to wonder how the bastards had known where to find us. Because they had known: they hadn't come up lucky and spotted the car or they would have parked where they could keep an eye on it. They had known we were inside the building, and they had been waiting for us to come out. At the same time the police who should have been there were mysteriously missing. Thinking about Charlie's phonecall, my blood ran chill.

FIVE

Only it didn't make sense. If my early misgivings about Charlie had been justified, then he might indeed have called Julian Barnes instead of Harry Marsh. All that he had said of his relationship with the Chief Inspector could have been lies – I'd heard it all from him, without corroboration. But then what was the purpose of that pantomime in my flat? The only possible explanation I could come up with was that somehow they expected me to lead them to Ben, whose anonymity represented the only promise of safety for either of us. In fact, if it were not the case that Charlie was a kind of fifth columnist for getting at Ben, the fail-safe device that he represented – that I had been so proud of – had proved about as efficacious as a mustard poultice for a compound fracture.

In the depths of the great stillness that I had suddenly become I gave silent thanks that I had sent Charlie on to the cafe before I called Ben at the hospital. Or had I? Hadn't he volunteered, even though it meant borrowing money? But that Cortina hadn't followed us, it hadn't searched for us through every street and car-park between here and the Skipley ring road, and if you believe in coincidences as long as it just happening to come down the motorway and stop here on the off-chance, I bet you believe in Father Christmas and leave apples for his reindeer too.

The conclusion that I had once again been betrayed seemed inescapable. In a Hollywood B-movie it would have looked like Charlie but turned out to be Harry Marsh. But this was not Chicago but the English Midlands. People like Harry Marsh might be slow, hidebound and ineffectual to a degree, but they were not corrupt. (People like Julian Barnes did not commit murder either, though.) And I had only Charlie's word for this improbable scenario of a Chief Inspector calling on the services of a Private Eye. Charlie Brown (an alias if ever I heard one!) on Julian's payroll was a much more credible concept; except that – except that – I didn't have any of the answers; I hated the questions like hell. I held my peace, and my breath.

The first dwelling our lights picked up was a low, mean cottage mouldering grimly under a corrugated tin roof. It did not look occupied, or for that matter habitable – a rotting relic of a time when farming was labour-intensive and count-less workers were employed to husband land and animals now managed by one family and several thousand pounds' worth of machinery.

Round the next bend loomed something more substantial, a two-storey brick farmhouse with barns and byres hemming in a squarish concrete yard. There was a light behind the kitchen door, another washing from a small uncurtained window in the side of the house out to a small orchard. The lane that entered the yard through an open gate at one end left through another opposite, proceeding presumably to serve other holdings in the same small valley. It was the sort of arrangement that would raise propertarian hackles in suburbia and never strike country-dwellers as anything out of the ordinary.

Charlie stopped the car and switched off the engine. The silence, after all the sound, was profound and subtly threatening. 'All right,' he said, freeing himself of his seat-belt, 'I'll go see if I can put an end to this nonsense.'

'No,' I said sharply – too sharply, he turned and stared at me, his hand frozen on the door. I opened my own door and quickly slid out. 'No, I'll go. It's dark, after all – the people here mightn't be too keen about letting in a young man they don't know from Adam, but nobody gets windy about middle-aged women.'

Charlie gave it a moment's thought then shrugged, subsiding in his seat. 'Okay.'

It made sense, of course, but that wasn't why I wanted to go myself. I wanted to talk to Marsh and make quite sure he had been informed of our predicament: if he had I would happily revert to trusting Charlie with my life. Also, if anyone was going to be caught sitting outside in the car, I didn't want it to be me.

The kitchen door sported a cast-iron knocker that predated Jethro Tull: I beat out a tattoo which was intended to convey a sense of urgency without frightening the life out of people who could hardly be accustomed to casual visitors, and ten seconds later a lantern above the door came on, spilling white light across the courtyard. The door was a cheerful cornflower blue, glossy with generations of paint, with a frosted glass panel behind which appeared a distorted shadow. A woman opened the door. Dogs barked half a house away.

I apologised for disturbing her and said we'd had an accident, which was true even if it was not comprehensive. I asked if I could use her telephone.

'Of course; come in,' she said. 'Are you hurt?'

'No, just shaken,' I said, which was also true enough.

She looked past me to the car, bright as a banana in the pool of light. She was about my age, taller and a good bit broader, a solidly capable woman who seemed to find nothing alarming in our arrival. Perhaps she was used to people falling off the motorway. 'Won't your husband come in too?'

'He's not – ' I began, but what the hell, if I started explaining we'd be standing there all night. 'He's not hurt

118

either. If I could just make the call – ?'

'Surely.' She showed me to an instrument in the hall that was probably installed about the time they chucked their horses out to grass to make room for their first tractor.

In the brief seconds it took the desk to ring through I thought, If Harry Marsh isn't in his office waiting for us it's because Charlie never spoke to him – called someone else instead, and if that's so I'm bolting the door, up-ending the kitchen table against the window and –

Harry Marsh snatched up his telephone and bellowed down it, 'Where the hell are you? I've mobiles searching half the county for you two. Why did you leave the service station? What the hell's going on?'

The relief turned my knees weak beneath me. I gave the woman an idiotic grin that only disposed her to worry about me more. I asked her, 'Where are we?'

She gave me the address and instructions for finding it which I passed on to Chief Inspector Marsh. I couldn't see his police cars taking the short-cut we had. He left me for a minute to despatch the information. When he got back he was calmer, quieter. 'They'll be with you in ten, fifteen minutes. Try to stay put this time. Are you all right?'

'Fine,' I said wearily, 'just fine. I've been sandbagged, tied up, knocked about; I've been threatened with three different deaths; I've had my car rammed and been driven down an embankment like the hairy part of a Big Dipper. I've been in a state of mortal terror since soon after lunchtime. As Mrs Lincoln said, apart from that I enjoyed the play fine.'

'And Charlie?'

I blinked, a little surprised at the tenor of his voice. 'Oh – er, he's fine too. Actually,' I said, warming to the subject, 'he's done a bloody good job. I don't how much he told you –'

I grew aware that he was no longer with me. In the background I could hear the froggy croak of an intercom. I couldn't hear what it said, and what I could hear of Marsh's response, faint as if across the room, sounded only terse and made no sense. When he came back it was with a rush of words, hard and rapid, delivered like machinegun-fire.

'Listen. They're after you. The car we sent arrived at the service station in time to see their tail-lights disappearing down the hill. They piled up trying to follow. The observer's got a broken leg. The driver's continuing on foot but he won't stop them single-handed and from behind. That farm: how many people are there?'

I didn't know. I asked the woman, trying to keep my voice level. But she knew something was wrong. 'Who is that?'

'Police. Please, how many?'

For the first time a flicker of fear crossed her strong face. 'Just me. There's a darts match in Crawley. They'll be back about eleven.'

'Me, Charlie and the farmer's wife,' I replied briefly into the phone.

'Christ,' swore Marsh, disgustedly. 'All right. Hide the car, then barricade yourselves in. Upstairs, behind the strongest door you can find. Lights out. Tell Charlie – '

'Hang on, hang on,' I begged him. 'I'll get Charlie to shift the car. It's right out front. Don't go away, will you?' There was nowhere to leave the handset down so I left the woman holding it.

I conveyed the content of my conversation with the Chief Inspector in three short sentences. Charlie sank his head on his forearms on the wheel; for only a moment. When he straightened up his face was set in hard, hollow lines. He didn't look young any more, or frightened, or anything but very tired. He was close to exhaustion, mental and physical, in that haunted, hunted state in which men make the terrible errors of judgement which get them branded as heroes or cowards, geniuses or fools, depending on luck and outcome. His reserves were gone: anything he had to do now would come out of his bones and blood and leave him diminished. I was sorry for him, sorry for what I'd brought him, but once again I was very glad to have him by me.

He reached for the ignition. 'Okay, I'll get this thing under cover – a barn or something. Do what Harry says, I'll be back in a – '

For a moment I couldn't think why he had stopped. Then I heard it too: a low growl of sound in the lane behind us. My heart gave a great lurch and the blood froze within me. My hand, talon-like with fear, clutched Charlie's arm through the open window. 'Oh dear God.'

Charlie wrenched the car into life. 'Go inside. Put out the lights. Lock the doors. Wait for Harry.' His voice was dead, hopeless and without passion. He pulled away while my arm was still through the folded window so that I had to jerk it back, shocked out of my cataplexy. The Citroen, spitting grit, accelerated through the far gate, its headlamps pulsing on the hedges like a beacon.

I ran inside and slammed and bolted the door behind me. 'The lights. Put out the lights!' I screamed to the woman, snatching back the phone. 'Lock everything.' In the sudden dark, knowing I was sobbing, I told Marsh, 'Charlie's gone. Taken the car. Drawing their fire. They'll crucify him. Do something, damn you – do something!'

There was a second's pause that ached like hours. Then: 'You're in the house. Are you safe there?'

I yelled, 'I don't know. I think so, for now. I think they'll chase the car – that's why he went. But he can't outrun them. They'll kill him, Marsh, and then they'll come back for me, and it will be your fault. Just make sure you nail the bastards afterwards. If there's enough evidence, that is.'

How Marsh replied to this bitter, monstrously unfair accusation I do not know. I wasn't listening. I was holding the telephone at arm's length and staring into the round face, like a dim moon in the darkness, of the woman beside me. '*What* did you say?'

'I said, I have a gun.'

I ought not to have been so surprised. All farms have guns – for foxes, rabbits, crows and the occasional visit of a pack of dogs up for an evening's sheep-worrying. It gave us a chance. No, it gave Charlie a chance; what it gave me was the opportunity to put myself back in the front line for him as he had done for me. 'Get it.' I thought only momentarily before deciding what to do with it.

I left Chief Inspector Marsh dangling on the end of the wire, squawking incomprehensibly. Through the frosted glass of the kitchen door I saw the big lights of the dark car arc across the yard, washing over the blind windows. With the glare on the house it paused long enough for me to see the woman creep down the stairs with something long and softly gleaming in her hands, then the engine note rose again and the bright beam marched on through the far gate, a scant minute behind Charlie.

The woman had remembered to bring a box of cartridges. 'I'm afraid I don't know how to load it.'

'I do.' I thumbed a cartridge into each barrel and pocketed half a dozen more, although I didn't expect to have time to reload. One shot for each of them: with a 12-bore, it should be enough. If they stood close enough together I could take them both with one round. 'Where does that lane go?'

'Only about a mile further,' she said, 'up to the old farm that was my husband's mother's. Nobody lives there now. We winter stock in the big barn.'

'Is there a short-cut?'

'No, but I can drive that lane faster than any of them. I'll take you up in the Land Rover.'

I stared at her. It was hard to see her expression but there was no mistaking the determination in her voice. 'I can't ask that. We've put you in danger already. Give me the keys –'

She shook her head firmly. She was the sort of woman you wouldn't give a second glance if you saw her in the street. I am constantly amazed and impressed by the depths of quiet courage that lurk in unexpected places. 'By the time you got the hang of it, you'd be too late to do any good. I'll take you. I'll drop you at the last bend and come back for the police.'

We ran across the yard and threw back the doors on the old drayhouse they used as a garage. The big square engine under the blue hood coughed into throaty life and I climbed up into the cab, settling the gun across my lap, as the lumbering vehicle powered in pursuit.

Her name was Mary Jackson. Apart from introducing ourselves we had little conversation on the short and noisy drive. She asked not why the men in the Cortina were chasing us but what they had done, which showed a nice perception, I thought.

'They killed two people. One was a friend of mine. When they realised I knew they tried to kill me too. Charlie – the boy in my car, I hardly knew him before tonight – got me away. They'll kick his head in for that.'

Mary Jackson took one broad hand off the shuddering wheel and patted the stock of the gun on my knees. 'They're outnumbered now.'

She left me where we had agreed, fifty yards from the old farm with the roof of the big barn a hard black silhouette against the softer darkness of the hill. We were near the top of the valley now, with the canopy of cloudwrack and the occasional stars hanging low above us. She turned the Land Rover in a gateway and thundered away back down the lane looking for the police driver.

We had seen nothing of either my car or the Cortina, but since the lane went no further I knew where they had to be. With the broken gun tucked under my arm, reassuring in its solid weight, I jogged the last steep stretch and dropped into a crouch behind a crumbling gatepost at the entrance to the yard. I stayed there a moment, my breath loud in my ears, taking stock.

Both cars were there, their headlamps illuminating the scene. They were stationary; both engines were still quietly ticking over; neither vehicle appeared to be occupied.

The Citroen had come to rest at an odd angle, its tail parked in the lower courses of a packed hayshed. The driver's door hung open, its self-closing properties defeated by the unmistakable slope of the yard. The Cortina was drawn across its bows, the length of it blocking any possibility of escape, its headlights shining through the gaping doors of the big barn which filled the right-hand side of the yard. I could hear the sounds of cattle, stamping and complaining. To the left lay the old farmhouse, more than half derelict now, and a range of low outbuildings which could have been stables, pigsties, chicken coops, or all those things by turns. There were no lights other than the car lights, and no sounds other than the cattle.

Better than evens they were in the barn. I snapped the gun closed and made for the light.

SIX

I could see why the Jacksons still used their mother's old barn. It was an enormous structure which would have cost a fortune to replace. The cattle – young stock, beef bullocks so far as I could judge – were in a series of long pens on either side of a central aisle. Opposite the open door on to the yard was another door, presumably giving access to a back field, but it was closed. Charlie must have tried to get out that way, running down the brilliant track of the beam, an unwilling performer in an unwanted spotlight, but fighting the unfamiliar bolts and latches he had run out of time and now they were beating the living daylights out of him.

They had been at it a scant few minutes, but you can do a lot to a man in a very short time if he has no way of defending himself. From the moment Chandos got his arms behind him Charlie was helpless, and Harwich had laid into him with all the frustration of the last couple of hours pent up in his big fists.

When they had killed Luke they had taken infinite trouble to leave no marks on him. That constraint no longer applied. After the day's adventures they could not hope to construct another plausible suicide: all they could do now was dispose of the witnesses and hope to ride out the storm. Left to their own devices these two might have preferred to run, but Barnes would hold them with an iron hand. He knew I hadn't been to the police since my suspicions had been

125

merest speculation. He didn't know I had spoken to Harry Marsh by telephone; he might have considered the possibility, but in the sheer panic of the afternoon comparatively little of my time was unaccounted for. He must have believed there was a good chance that the Skipley police had never heard his name. While there was any chance of saving his career he would bluff it out; and with me dead the most he should have to explain was a very casual friendship dating back to medical school. That was why Charlie was still alive: so he could tell them where to find me.

Actually, all they had to do was look towards the gaping door. Chandos was even facing me, Charlie's drooping head no obstacle between us, but he was too engrossed in what he was doing to glance up and I slipped through the door and advanced up the aisle on the edge of the beam, dark against the stamping animal darkness, a raging calm behind a double-barrelled 12-bore.

In their enthusiasm to repay him for his interference – with me dead over a vial of diamorphine they could have been back at their clinic and going on with their lives by now – I think they had forgotten that they needed Charlie not only alive but lucid if they were to wring from him the information they required. After the hammering he'd taken I doubt if he knew where he was, let alone where I was. He hung limp in Chandos' grasp, his chin on his chest, his long legs buckled at the knees: without the big hands holding him he could not have stood. His shirt was torn open and his throat and chest were slick with perspiration. His skin was fishbelly white in the glare of the headlamps, except for an angry red area like a target in the centre of his midriff. As I watched, advancing softly, Harwich landed another hefty punch in his middle that doubled Charlie over and drove a grunt of animal agony from him.

Chandos straightened him up from behind, lifting his head by a handful of straw-coloured hair. His voice, reaching me over the milling sounds of the uneasy cattle, was vicious, laced with an atavistic hatred. 'Where is she? Here? At that house? *Where?*'

In the harsh light Charlie's face had the martyred, mediaeval look of a hung Christ, parchment pale, translucent as porcelain. His eyes were almost closed, the long lashes wet with sweat or tears, his lips parted. His lower lip was broken and blood ran down his chin. There was no fear left in his face, and no understanding: all that was left to him was pain. Guilt twisted in my gut like a knife. When the pain stopped he would sink into the waiting oblivion, a dark and aching slumber like a hole in the ground where his hurt body would either yield up its life or begin the slow, miraculous business of healing. But the pain was not over yet. Harwich powered another murderous blow in under his ribs.

'*Where?*'

'Here.'

My voice, low and about as ladylike as a cobra's, brought Harwich spinning round. The sight of the big gun in my arms shocked Chandos into dropping his burden: noiselessly, bonelessly, Charlie folded to the cement floor and lay still. I had a clear shot at them. I needed almost no provocation to take it.

Caught out in their crime, like small boys caught tormenting a cat, guilty-eyed and with more hands than they knew what to do with, they seemed quite pathetically startled. Uncertain what to do or say they froze silently in their brutal, awkward poses.

Somehow – I can't now remember quite how but I remember the impulse – there was a way in which I could almost feel sorry for them. If Julian Barnes had needed their muscle, they had needed his brain, his wit, far more. It's an odd word to use, but for all their savagery they were innocents, incompletely equipped for the complex business of living. Perhaps it was only bad luck that had put them under the aegis of so unprincipled a man as Julian: perhaps Dr Schweitzer would have made missionaries of them. They were young men from privileged backgrounds, qualified in a good and honourable profession, with every hope of success and prosperity, but as rounded, rational, responsible human beings they were non-starters. They were moral defectives, as intellectually gifted and as capable of discriminate judgement as a couple of hand-grenades.

Even so, I might have had difficulty reconciling these slack-faced, stiff-limbed marionettes with the painstaking, perfectionist murderers of my friend Luke had it not been for the crumpled figure at their feet of the latest unfortunate to get in their way, beaten systematically senseless in their absolute determination to escape the consequences of their actions.

I had a sudden revelation, shocking in its import and its clarity, that despite everything we purported to believe to the contrary it was the practice of medicine itself, with its preoccupation with frail and damaged bodies and with pain, that was the great brutaliser, the thief of sensitivity and humility – for how else could one mortal being presume to cut into the living body of another? Perhaps what we choose to call professional detachment is in reality only the hardening of the spirit against suffering, a callousness which made possible both vital surgical procedures and the sort of things these two had done and others before them. Doctors live with pain and death more than soldiers: why should we be immune to their effects? If we can be tempered, we can also be corrupted.

I surfaced from my untimely reverie with a new perception, a sense of outrage at the trick long perpetrated and unsuspected, and the awareness that there would be more appropriate times to think about it. Harwich was emerging from his own state of shock and had seen the glazed eyes that signalled mine. So that he should clearly understand that the moment for taking advantage was gone I said, softly and distinctly, 'There is a policeman on his way up here. If you do exactly as I tell you and nothing more, there is every likelihood that you will be here to greet him when he arrives. But if you cause me an instant's concern, I shall turn you into a nasty smear on the back wall. What's more, I shall enjoy doing it.'

Down among the feet Charlie was suffering the slow realisation that he was still in the land of the living. The heap he had become when Chandos let go of him uttered a low groan and, like a rather lanky tortoise, pushed out limbs and a heavy, bleary head. I said his name. His eyes came up, unfocused, narrowed against the light. 'What?'

'You okay?'

There was a moment's heavy silence while he sat on the cement floor, considering. Then he said, 'Of course I'm bloody not;' which rather suggested that, give or take a split lip and the odd cracked rib, he probably was.

'Come over here then.'

He blinked some comprehension into his eyes and looked round. I could see him taking in the looming proximity of the large young men, their sudden inactivity, and the long and faintly gleaming thing in my arms; and indeed me, whom he had left in safety half way down the valley. 'Ah,' he said pontifically. He started getting up. It was a long hard climb.

If you watch any amount of television you'll have seen people doing some odd things with guns. They push their hats back with them, blow down the barrels, shove them into pockets and hit one another on the head with them, apparently oblivious of the possible consequences of such cavalier behaviour. And from time to time you'll see someone threaten someone else by prodding him in the middle with a double-barrelled shotgun. Take it from me, this is equally not a good idea. It is not a good idea from the point of view of the recipient of the prod, because if it goes off even accidentally a big gun at point blank range will make a large hole where there used to be a small intestine. But it is also not a good idea from the gunman's point of view, because he is putting within the compass of his enemy's reach the one thing which enables him to dominate the situation. Grabbing it, with all the risks attendant on that, may seem a desperate measure, but people with shotguns pointed at their middles are commonly in desperate straits and may consider, if they give it any thought at all, that they have little or nothing left to lose.

I did not prod Chandos with the 12-bore, but I did allow it to stray unconscionably close to those prodigious hands. Blessed by fate with the means of turning them and their owner into meat-loaf, I had forgotten just how dangerous those hands were. I was worrying about Charlie: he was too close to Harwich for my peace of mind, and if he ever succeeded in getting off his knees he would block a line of fire I was anxious to preserve. Thinking to move them back to where they could do no harm, I took a step towards Chandos, who was nearest, waving the barrels significantly at his expansive tweed abdomen. 'Against the wall.'

He couldn't have thought what he was going to do, there was no time. He grabbed the barrels with both hands and snatched the gun out of my grasp, the trigger-guard skinning my knuckle as it went. Swinging like an axe, the stock of the solid weapon caught Charlie as he rose and flung him bodily against the planks of the stock-pen; then it whistled back in my direction.

That was his mistake. He had only to hold the gun out of my reach – and I'm five foot two: he must have been about six foot four – while he reversed it to gain total command of the situation and the time to think out his next move carefully and without pressure. Instead, carried away perhaps by the success of his initiative, he tried to fell me too with the returning flail of the wood and steel pendulum. I saw it coming, timed the swing and caught the stock as it reached me. Without trying to wrest it away from him I found a trigger and pulled it.

Even in the big barn the noise was deafening. The penned cattle reacted to it with bellows of fear and a great trampling of movement away from the central aisle. Chandos seemed to have disappeared entirely, leaving me once more holding the gun. After a moment I located what was left of him, in the drainage gutter where it cut under the back wall. He had been thrown yards by a dense pattern of shot propelled by a massive charge only an arm's length away, and there remained not the least shadow of a doubt but that he was dead. It would have killed him a dozen times over.

I found myself holding the gun, quite calmly, facing Harwich.

I cannot explain what happened next. I cannot justify it, and I feel no particular urge to try. The police put it down to shock and fear, which made sense enough, but that wasn't the reason. I was just sick and tired of being hunted. They had murdered Luke, tried to kill me and beaten Charlie to within inches of his life. Even in the face of a gun they had refused to concede defeat: I had been forced to kill one of them to save myself. Now the other was waiting his chance and I was still in danger. I had no idea how long I should have to wait for relief. This near salvation I was taking no chances.

I watched Harwich's eyes until I saw in them an embryonic appreciation of what I intended. He thought about it, dismissed it, couldn't quite get it out of his mind, thought about it more seriously, accepted the possibility, accepted finally the horrid truth: that his activities had reduced me to an unscrupulous cold-bloodedness comparable only with his own. When I saw in his eyes the knowledge that I was going to kill him – like a mad dog, without mercy or compunction or regret – I let him have the second barrel.

131

Standing there afterwards, thinking I must get round to putting the gun down sometime, waiting for some sense of what I had done to catch up with me, I grew aware that Charlie had not come back the way he should have done. You don't expect a man to bounce up from a toppling like that, especially after the sort of evening Charlie had had, but I would have thought that the explosion of two gun-shots scant feet from his ear, that had set the crowded animals milling like an imminent stampede, would have helped to focus his attention. Thinking that perhaps he had been stunned, by the blow or by the fall, I laid the gun aside and went over and knelt beside him where he sprawled along the foot of the pen, mostly on his side with his face turned from me.

'Charlie?'

I knew something was wrong the moment I touched him, feeling the awful tension in his long muscles which I had expected to find slack with concussion. When I turned him to me, my hands rough with sudden urgency, I saw what it was. He couldn't breathe. By accident or design – the former, I think, there was no time for the latter – the stock of the shotgun, swinging like a morning-star with all the power of Chandos' big frame and desperation behind it, had caught him full in the throat, fracturing his larynx and closing his windpipe. His eyes were terrified, white-wild; even as I bent to him they began to glaze and roll up and his clutching hands lost their purpose as consciousness failed him. I fastened my mouth on his open mouth and tried to force air past the blockage but there was no response, no sense of yielding. He was suffocating, and in another minute or so he would be dead. I jerked to my feet and ran like hell.

With almost no one left to move them the cars were as I had seen them last. I hefted a half-brick through one of the Citroen's frog-eye headlamps. I would have preferred to smash one of the Cortina's headlamps and save myself money, but I needed their light. Among the shards that rained out I found a long piece, razor-edged, and wrapped my handkerchief round one end. Then I threw up the bonnet and hacked four inches of plastic tube out of the windscreen washer. Then I ran back through the barn – counting, all the time counting.

Of all the life-saving operations known to medical science, none is simpler or more effective than a tracheotomy. All you really need is skill: the tools, a scalpel and an airway, are so simple that they can at need be improvised. Asepsis is nice, but there are things you can do about infection. Death is more permanent.

Charlie was just about aware of me when I dropped back at his side. I lugged him into a better light and got his sliding attention by the simple expedient of slapping his face.

'Charlie,' I said, and my voice was hard and firm to go with the firm, steady hands and not with the tiny shrilling panic deep inside my brain where I knew it had been too long, I wasn't good enough, I'd do it wrong, it was too dangerous. I pressed on, willing myself strength. 'You know who I am. You know I'm a doctor. You're going to be all right. Do two things. Trust me. And keep still.'

I didn't know if he had understood or not. There was no more time. With the tube in my teeth for safe keeping I bent over him like a vampire and cut his throat with my glass dagger.

3

ONE

Also rather like a vampire, Harry Marsh with his raincoat
flying flapped up the front steps of the hospital, batted aside
the glass doors and flared to a halt in the centre of the tile and
vinyl waiting area in a swirl of black gabardine and wild
looks.

For a moment, glancing up from my plastic cup of syn-
thetic coffee, I did not recognise him. Out from behind his
desk he looked taller and younger, or at least more animated.
Like an agitated vampire he turned on his heel in the centre
of the labour-saving floor until he spotted me in my quiet
corner. I raised a hand in reluctant acknowledgement and he
stalked over, stiff with some intensity of feeling. I thought we
were in for a scene. My heart, already low from the leaching
away of the evening's high emotions, hugging itself in a
slowly deepening morass of pale grey depression, made the
small effort necessary to sink still lower.

Returning from a reconnaissance of the vending machines,
my escort – the police driver who had turned up just seconds
too late to be any use at all and had ridden back to Skipley in
the ambulance which came for his observer, Charlie and me
– moved to intercept him. When he realised who it was he
suddenly thought of something else demanding his attention.

Looming over me, even quaking slightly, the Chief Inspector demanded, 'Where is he? Is he all right?'

I had known Harry Marsh long enough by now, in ex-

134

perience if not in actual months, so that I did not expect anxious enquiries after my well-being, or apologies for his failure to protect me, or even non-committal commiserations. He was not a gracious man; which was a pity, because he did not strike me as being all that good at his job either and people should try to be one or the other. So I did not anticipate much by way of a greeting; but what I got was so much less than even basically civil, and incomprehensible as well, that I nettled.

'Two are dead and two are damaged,' I said coldly. 'You'll have to be more specific.'

'Charlie,' he said thickly, fisting his hands in his pockets to stop them sneaking off and misbehaving on their own account.

I could have answered his clumsiness with ripostes of barbed wit to reduce him to dumb anger if not to rage. But you don't tease frightened children or hurt animals, and whatever the reason for his distress it was genuine and it made him equally unfair game. I relented. 'Charlie's fine; or at least, he will be. He took a bit of a beating and he ended up with a fractured larynx.' I touched my throat to show him. 'I had to open an airway for him. He's in theatre now, getting it tidied up. A couple of months hence he'll have nothing to show for it but a rather dinky little scar.'

The seat beside me, that was the driver's before he went off to Egon Ronay the soup dispenser, was vacant. Marsh dropped into it like a hod of bricks. His eyes were appalled. 'You mean, you operated on him? How – what with – ?'

I smiled. 'With extreme difficulty. With a piece of glass and some plastic tubing from the remains of my car. And with complete success.'

He sat there, breathing heavily, for a minute while the extreme tension of his square body eased and his nerves unknotted themselves. Then he pushed his legs out in front of him and, crossing them at the ankles, said glumly into his chest, 'God knows what my mum's going to say.'

I had that ominous sensation of time slowing down, of the skin growing cool and the mind still and the face stiffening in a terrifying vacancy of expression, that you get when you suddenly realise that the man in your surgery, with his trouserlegs rolled up and his socks rolled down to show where the dahlias bite his ankles, is in fact quite mad and also closer to your letter-opener than you are to your telephone.

I looked at the policeman with as near nothing in my eyes as I could contrive and said carefully, 'If you think she'll be upset, perhaps it would be better not to tell her.'

He looked at me much as I was looking at him. 'What?'

I explained reasonably, 'Old ladies are easily frightened. You don't have to tell her everything about your work, do you?'

Something alarming was happening to him. A little like a seizure and a little like a minor earthquake, it sent tremors through his big frame and colour into his face which had been the shade of old concrete under the unflattering fluorescent tubes. When it finally broke it was a laugh: no mere polite smirk such as you can simulate in most circumstances but a deep, insistent, full-bellied laugh that squeezed tears from his eyes and made people look at him. 'The silly bastard,' he managed moistly at last, 'he hasn't told you.'

I was relieved, of course, that he wouldn't be going for my neck after all, but I was still totally perplexed. 'Told me what?'

'Charlie's my brother. He's a stupid son-of-a-bitch, he dresses like a superannuated hippy and makes his living in a manner only marginally more respectable than playing piano in a bordello, but he's my kid brother and I love him, and when it came over the radio he'd been hurt – ' He broke off and shook his head, then chuckled deeply to himself again. 'Don't tell her if you think she'll be upset!'

'Brother?' I stammered, so taken aback I was barely

within shouting distance.

'Half-brother,' he explained, 'hence the different names. But my mum is Charlie's mum too. She says she's 61 and only ever made two mistakes. Old ladies are easily frightened – oh, she'll love that!'

He dissolved once more in an excess of hilarity that was at least part hysteria, and finally for lack of anything better to do I joined him. The tears and the laughter did us both good. When they dried up at length we talked like normal people.

'I thought you didn't believe me.'

'Belief was never the issue. You gave me nothing to act on. No, that's not quite fair, you narrowed it down to the entire medical profession and thought it might have had something to do with a book that wasn't there. I don't think Sherlock Holmes could have done much with that lot.'

'I told you it was something to do with kidneys.'

'So you did. You even turned out to be right. But it was a lucky shot. As things stood at close of play today, no court in the county would have issued search warrants for the premises of every hospital and every doctor working with kidneys inside a thirty mile radius of Skipley, and that's what it would have taken to get at Barnes.'

Today. Had all these insane things really happened today? Was it only this afternoon that I saw Julian, this evening that his people tried to kill me, tonight that I killed them? It seemed half a lifetime ago. Dear God, it was only a fortnight since Luke died, and already the cut flowers were withering on my memory of him.

'I traced it to him,' I pointed out stiffly, reluctant in my heart to concede what my head had known all along: that in all the circumstances there was little more he could have done.

'Not strictly true,' he said. 'You concluded it was Barnes and challenged him with it. Because of the relationship between you which he believed would prevent you from

137

informing on him, he admitted it. If you had persuaded me to accuse him he would not have admitted it. He would have invited me to prove it, and I would have been spectacularly incapable of doing so. Without wishing to denigrate your talents as a detective, I would have to ascribe your impressive record in this particular case to your privileged position as intimate and confidante of both the victim and the criminal.'

'Privileged.' I let out a little snort of laughter. 'Yeah. That's just what it felt like.' We grinned at each other in the new companionship of mutual understanding. I said, 'Then what about Charlie?'

'Exactly because I couldn't wind it up quickly, I wanted someone to keep an eye on you. The best I could have done officially was a squad car calling by twice a day. But Charlie had a quiet week or two: he agreed to move in and be handy in case you started getting visitors and were too bloody-minded to let on. The idea, mind you, was that he call me, not that he take them on like sodding Superman.'

'If he'd called you that time you'd have had nothing to do but pick up the body.' Irritation surged. 'Why didn't you *tell* me?'

'I didn't tell you at the start because I judged you were in no mood to accept personal favours from me.' He cranked up an eyebrow interrogatively. I nodded meekly. At that point I'd have told him where to stick his little brother. 'And I imagine that Charlie didn't tell you later because he finds it as embarrassing having a policeman for a brother as I do having a private eye.'

'Security consultant,' I murmured.

'*I* am a security consultant,' he said with dignity. 'There is nothing that people like Charlie can do that the police can't do better, and what's more for free.'

It sounded like a precis of a five-year-old argument. If Charlie had been there he would doubtless have made the same retort he always did, and as it always did the argument would have tailed off in grunts and brotherly insults without resolving anything. There was probably a lot in what Marsh said, but as things had turned out he could hardly expect me to agree with him. As things had turned out, indeed, he might have been better preserving a tactful silence.

'What about Barnes?'

Marsh looked at his watch. 'He should be hearing a knock on his door any time now.'

'You'll charge him with murder?'

'Murder and attempted murder. With your testimony and Charlie's – Charlie will be able to give evidence?' he asked with sudden anxiety.

'He'll have to write his statement, but given the length of time it takes you people to get a case to court he'll be able to sing to the jury if need be.'

Marsh grinned. I was reluctant to wipe that smile off his face but I too had concerns which demanded prompt attention. 'What about me?'

'What about you?'

'Chief Inspector, I shot two men dead. One of them gave me no choice – it was self-defence, pure and simple. The other one – I don't know. He had tried to kill me, several times, and Charlie, and I'm pretty sure he'd have tried again. But at the precise moment that I shot him he was just standing there. He was just damn well standing there –'

Only when his broad square hands gripped my shoulders did I realise that I had begun to shake and that my voice was breaking. I don't know why. I did not regret what I had done. It is probably true to say that if I had done anything else Charlie would have died, for though I might have realised he was in trouble there was no way I could have performed a tracheotomy while still keeping the shotgun a safe protection between us and Harwich. That may not have made what I did morally right, but on a practical level it meant that a bad man's death had bought a good man's life. I felt no qualms about it. Only I couldn't seem to stop shaking.

Marsh said, as slowly and clearly as if he was talking to an idiot child, 'We'll have to take a statement, of course. When you're feeling a bit better. You can get your solicitor up if you like. But quite honestly, in view of the background and everything that you'd been through in the previous few hours, I can't see the DPP wanting you charged. Even if he did no jury would convict you, and even if they did no judge would punish you. Such as it is I'll stake my pension that once you've signed your statement you'll hear no more about it.'

I said, rather formally, 'Thank you.'

He pressed a neatly folded handkerchief into my hands. I did not know why and stared at it, perplexed, until he leaned close enough not to be overheard and murmured, 'You're crying.'

I didn't want to go back to Mr Pinner's house that night, and anyway the Scenes of Crime boys were taking photographs and measurements and probably bits of fluff and samples of carpet dust too – again: you'd have thought they could look up the results of their first scrutiny and save themselves a trip.

Harry Marsh booked me into an hotel. We were about to leave the hospital when I finally thought of Ben Sawyer. Our last exchange had been in the thick of the pursuit, when I called from the motorway. Though the worst had then seemed to be over, I knew he would have been waiting for another call, in the absence of which he would have been worrying himself sick for hours. Though I was longing for bed I couldn't for shame let the night go by entirely without letting him know I was safe.

I tried the hospital, finally got him at home. But he did not sound he had done much sleeping.

'Clio, where are you? Are you all right? What's happening?'

'Nothing, now.' I stifled a yawn compounded of reaction and a bone-deep weariness. 'It's all over. You'll be getting a box of bits in the morning that was once two large young men on the staff of the Schaefer Clinic, and the police are on their way up there for the Godfather right now. I'll see you tomorrow.'

'Clio!' He sounded like a child sent to bed before the end of the cartoons, while the Coyote still looks like getting the Road Runner. 'What happened? Are you sure you're all right? You don't really sound it. Tell me where you are. Do you want me to come over?'

'Tomorrow, Ben. I'll see you tomorrow. I'll tell you everything there is to know, tomorrow.'

TWO

For ease of communication until his throat should heal up I bought Charlie a magic slate. The toyshops sell them for children: you scribble your picture or message in a trail of magnetised iron filings imprisoned behind a plastic screen. You can go on writing and erasing and writing and erasing as long as you can think up anything to say.

The woman in the toyshop demonstrated. This was the day after Armageddon. Post-trauma reaction had left me unusually voluble, and to fill a silence while she wrapped the thing I said, 'It's for a young friend of mine who's in hospital.'

'Nothing serious, I hope?' I assured her he was on the mend. 'And what age is the little chap?'

'About twenty-four.'

She didn't blink; the sympathetic smile never so much as wavered. 'Do you suppose he'd like some Plasticine as well?' she said.

Flouting visiting hours shamelessly I took the thing round to Charlie and we – that is, we – well, okay, we played with it. There is nothing like a close encounter of the last kind to project you into a second childhood.

Charlie looked good. To me: his mother would have been appalled. His face was all the hues of a jaundiced rainbow, one eye was closed and his lower lip was swollen grotesquely out to one side. His ribs were strapped up, great blue bruises leaking above and below, and in the hole in his throat were two tubes, one of which tended to pop out when he tried to laugh. Tracheotomy patients aren't supposed to be in any laughing mood. Above the plumbing a dressing covered the surgery to his larynx. He looked like a reject Android. He was alive. He looked wonderful.

We were engaged in a rather curious game of Botticelli. I don't know why we felt compelled to play word games, or what was suddenly wrong with noughts and crosses, but there it is: the perversity of the human spirit. When the pace hotted up and the excitement started getting to us I was trying to write my answers and Charlie to speak his. In the spluttering confusion thus created Harry Marsh shouldered through the door and, silently, hands in pockets, stood at the foot of the bed and regarded us morosely.

Charlie, lifting an eyebrow in silent enquiry, eased his long body into a shallow S-bend below the sheets, to accommodate me on one side of his bed and his brother on the other. Harry sniffed briefly and sat down.

It was the first time I had seen them together and I observed them with interest. There were nineteen years between them: Harry started his police career the year Charlie was born. Harry lived in the Midlands and Charlie lived with their mother in the West Country; they met maybe once in six months. They were of different generations, different outlooks, quite different styles: all they had in common was a half-set of genes. It didn't matter. They had a sense of family that went wider and deeper than miles and years and differences of opinion. It showed in the unconscious flick of Harry's eyes, every few seconds, checking that Charlie was still there and still fine, and in the almost dog-like pleasure with which Charlie responded to his name on his brother's lips. In a cynical old world it was nice how much they cared about each other.

Harry jerked his head at the invalid and spoke to me.

143

'How's he feeling now?'

I said to Charlie, 'He wants to know how you're feeling now.'

Charlie wrote on his board 'OK' and showed it to me.

I said to Harry, 'He says he feels OK.'

Harry glared at the pair of us. 'You're as daft as one another,' he grunted.

Charlie wrote: 'You look like someone pinched the pea from your whistle.'

Harry sniffed again and shrugged himself deeper into his raincoat, although the ward was as warm and sweetly stuffy as wards always are. 'I've got bad news.'

My heart paused, turned over and raced on. I felt the colour drain from my face. 'They're going to do me for shooting those bastards.'

'No, not that,' Harry said hurriedly. He reached across Charlie's legs to touch my arm with clumsy reassurance. 'I told you, I don't think you've anything to worry about. I might hear a few pointed questions about how my disreputable little brother came to be involved, but it isn't even that. It's Barnes. We've lost him.'

I don't know how I had managed to forget about Julian Barnes. Perhaps because when it finally came to open conflict the enemy had been two other people. When your back is against the wall your thinking suffers, loses cohesion: the bits that are of immediate and vital importance are very clear, preternaturally so, so clear that the time they are couched in slows down perceptibly to leave you all the leisure in the world to do what needs doing; but the background fades, becomes dislocated, and afterwards it takes time to come back. I had thought – not sensibly, not with reason, but instinctively, at gut level – that when Chandos and Harwich were bloody garbage, sending the penned cattle wild with the stench of the charnelhouse, it was finished. I knew there was still Barnes, but my mind – its processes disturbed as a flung stone disturbs a pool, shattering the images reflected there – could not seem to keep the fact in focus. I had forgotten him. And I felt guilty, terribly guilty, as though in some indefinable way it was because I had forgotten him that the police had lost him.

In the same way I discovered, sitting on Charlie's bed in an atmosphere gone suddenly still and grey as a desolation of the soul, that I had somehow contrived to forget what it was all for. I had forgotten Luke, and his dying that had been the start of this, the reason for it. Despair gripped me with cold hands. I could not remember his face. Dear God, his face! – I loved him for fifteen years and now I couldn't remember what he looked like. The sense of bereavement rekindled, rising about me like wreathing smoke. Leave me that, I begged silently, in bitterness and grief, but it was too late. The last of Luke had gone, unnoticed in the flurry of the contest, and awareness of the loss turned to ashes the sweet relief that was my own survival. It was true that, if success must be measured in absolutes, I had won rather than lost the battle; but it was a shallow, insubstantial victory. Luke was no less dead.

I was alive, but no more alive than if I had left the inquiry to the professionals and gone home to suffer and at length come through a normal mourning, and then Charlie too would be safe at home instead of breathing hospital air through a hole in his throat. Perhaps Harry Marsh was not the world's greatest policeman and Julian Barnes' crime would have gone unsuspected; so that instead of spending six month on the run and the rest of his life making a fortune changing faces in South America he would have stayed to winkle out the gremlins in his Artificial Implantable Kidney thus saving countless lives and vastly improving countless others. All I had achieved, it seemed, was the death of two rather foolish and impressionable young men who had not the talent, the application, the patience or the stamina to succeed in their profession by conventional means and so consented to Burke-and-Hare for a man whose eminence was unchallenged in return for some reflection of that glory. They were not good men – probably they deserved to be killed more than I deserved to be made a killer – but I still harboured the rankling suspicion that they had been more easily led than evil. Julian had manipulated them with the same consummate skill that he displayed in theatre, making them as much his tools as his scalpels and his clamps. They lacked the character to escape his machinations and had neither the conscience nor the imagination to shrink from the consequences: he had used them, and then cynically used the time their deaths had bought him to evade arrest and so make a mockery of all the suffering, all the grief.

Charlie had scrawled the letters 'HOW?' and underlined them, heavily.

Also heavily, Harry shrugged. 'Just lucky, I guess. We thought we had him. One squad went to his house and one to the clinic. The wife – ' Wife? How curious that he should have been married; how much more so that I should not have wondered – 'said he hadn't come home and let us look round the house. But the clinic said he'd left quarter of an hour earlier to make the five-minute drive home. We finally found his car round the back of the railway station. He could be anywhere by now. Nobody remembered what train he got on. We put out an alert but you can't make much of a search on that basis. He'll probably try to leave the country. We wired a photograph to airports and docks, but if a man like that can't call up a favour from a friend with a yacht or a light aircraft he hasn't belonged to the right clubs all these years. He could be half way to Buenos Aires already.'

I sucked in a deep breath and stared at the treetops, showing their first green through the window behind Charlie's head, trying to come to terms with how I felt. My emotions were in chaos. Why was I hunting him? The man had been my friend – until he killed a better friend and tried to kill me, and made me a killer too. Did I hate him? I could not have said with absolute conviction that I did. I had set out to destroy him and I had succeeded – captive or free, his reputation was gone for good. There would be no Nobel Prize now. If he ever found a way to finish his work on the AIK it would be impossible for him to publish in his own name. One way and another he would make enough money to live comfortably in the places he was bound for, but that loss of regard he would find hard to bear.

Was I satisfied? I did not know. Was my vendetta prompted only by personal fury, or could I delegate some of it to professional outrage? I didn't know that either, and perhaps it did not matter. Finally, if I had had Julian where I had young Harwich, would the outcome have been the same? My instincts warred together, half seeming to argue that, for the sake of our old friendship, I should be content to see the matter ended so, while the other half wanted – because of that very friendship betrayed – nothing less than absolute justice untempered by any more mercy than he himself had dispensed.

Unable to find a consensus within the jumble of my own feelings I turned on Harry Marsh. I stood up and did not look at him. I did not shout – it might have been less cruel if I had. I said only, grimly and quietly, 'You're responsible for this. If you'd acted on what I told you, you could have stopped him. You could have had the three of them in custody now instead of two on the slab and one on the run. It's thanks to you that Charlie's been beaten within an inch of his life; and it's nothing short of a miracle that it's not his body and mine cluttering up Ben Sawyer's morgue right now. By your incompetence you are directly responsible for everything that has happened since Luke Shaw was murdered; and you thought that was suicide.'

Letting the scorn drip from my tongue like icy venom I

gave him one long sideways look and then left, straight-backed with spurious dignity and already feeling like a worm. As the door swung close behind me I saw from the corner of my eye that Harry had made to follow me and that Charlie had detained him with a hand on his arm.

I don't know what it is about behaving like a rat. You'd think that as soon as you realised you were doing it you'd be falling over yourself to be sweetness and light, but are you? Not a bit of it, your first instinct is to find somebody else you can be even more of a rat to. I sought out the Department of Pathology to go and make Ben's life a misery.

They had given the dead a surprisingly pleasant corner of the hospital compound, semi-detached from the main buildings and screened by a row of poplars. It was their heads I had seen from Charlie's bedside: there were a couple of dozen of them, tall slender pencils just beginning to green, sap vibrant with a spring whose promise they must have had on good authority since there were no other signs of it yet.

Somebody paged Ben for me and, rather than go back into the hospital with its smells and its claustrophobia that depressed me even when I worked in one, I asked him to walk with me under the trees. Within half a minute he started to turn blue: he had not come prepared for a hike. Why he did not nip back for his coat I did not understand, and it irritated me; and, irritated, I did not take the obvious and humane step of prompting him but determined to let him shiver it out if he lacked the initiative to get it without being told. I was not responsible for him: he was a grown man and I was neither his wife nor his mother. See what I mean about quantum escalation of rat-like behaviour? We walked beneath the trees, and Ben shivered and I glowered, and he said, 'What happened last night?'

I scowled and my lip wrinkled up, though I don't know what it was supposed to signify. Shock had left me in a treacherous state of near-normality, so that people who were admiring the way I had come through the events of the last hours and days were startled when I suddenly threw a false reaction, laying into Harry Marsh or sneering at poor shivering Ben. It would have been easier if I had kept dissolving in tears: they would have known how to cope with that. But I was always more inclined to yell than to cry, and they should both have known that you don't escape unscathed from that kind of trauma even if I had appeared to. Charlie knew; but Charlie had been there. Charlie, when the time came for him to face the real world again, would experience the same kind of difficulties readjusting. Maybe he would cry when people expected him to yell. Damn them all. We were entitled to our scars.

I said, 'The bastards came after me. Two tame gorillas of Barnes': I saw them with him, when I went there. They were waiting for me when I got back to the flat, setting up another suicide – diamorphine if I co-operated, and if I didn't they were going to pour bleach down my gullet.'

Ben's milk-blue face drained paler still and something more than cold shuddered through his frame. There was a certain satisfaction in rocking him with something I was already coming to terms with.

'They'd have had me, too, but for the boy downstairs. You remember Charlie? – I was right about him, he was planted on me, not by Barnes but by your friend Harry Marsh. There was a car chase like something out of a bad movie, they wrecked the Citroen, they beat up Charlie and I blew them away with a borrowed shotgun.' I paused, considering. 'I don't think I've left anything important out; those are the highlights, anyway. Except that this morning it transpires that the police, moving with their customary stealth, speed and efficiency, mounted brilliantly effective simultaneous raids on an empty office and an empty house' – I didn't mention the surprising Mrs Barnes, who would have spoiled the flow of my rhetoric – 'while the thinking man's Crippen was already exploring the surviving intricacies of British Rail with his Red Rover clutched in his hot little hand. They've no idea where to look for him, and between you, me and that squirrel the general feeling appears to be that when he finally surfaces it'll be within spitting distance of the Plaza de Belgrano.'

We walked in silence, pace for measured pace, under the trees where the air was cool and still and the gravel path whispered discreetly under our feet. Ben did not look at me. When I looked at him he had his hands in his pockets and his eyes, unfocused, on the roofs of the main building as if he were contemplating some eternal pathological verity. Only the small intense frown gathered between his brows and the working of a rogue muscle high up in his cheek suggested that our perambulation was not a mere casual taking in of the air. Walking silently at my side he looked tall and cold and frail somehow, and against my earlier inclinations I began to feel anxious about him. I jogged his elbow. 'Are you all right?'

He cast me a quick, sick grin. 'Hell's teeth, Clio, *I* don't know. Good God, what a tale. At least it's all over now. Are *you* all right?'

'Me? I'm fine. You should see the other two guys. Oh – you probably have.'

He stopped and stared down at me. His eyes were shocked and sad, but they also contained an understanding that the caustic humour, like the rattiness before, came more from the mouth than from the heart. Something that was more warmth than colour rose in his face and he reached out for me.

'Come here.'

Carefully avoiding my bruised arm, he held me against him. We stood there like a couple of idiots, a mismatched pair of wrestlers in a contortion of a clinch, listening to each other's hearts and breathing, the sheer physical closeness

150

unknotting nerves and muscles and letting ease seep in where there had been only deep tension.

And perhaps it was part of that letting-down process, the relaxing of pent-up emotions and reactions, so that normal channels of thought became passable once again. Or perhaps I had known before, subconsciously, because of something that Charlie had said and something that I had done and now something that Ben had done. Anyway, when at length he put me down and grinned sheepishly at me, I met his eyes with a kind of calm, clear impassivity and my voice was even.

'Did you help them to kill him, Ben, or was your role only to ensure that they got away with it?'

THREE

'I don't believe in private medicine,' he said, gazing into his folded hands. 'I never have. I consider it a drain on resources of time and talent, and to some extent money, which the National Health needs to provide a proper service. It could be so much better than it is – it should be, we promise proper medical care in return for the large quantities of money ordinary people pay us, regardless of their individual needs and inclinations, but we don't deliver it. We let people struggle on for years in pain and serious disability when we have medical and surgical procedures capable of transforming their lives in a couple of weeks. We let people die when we could restore them to reasonable health if we had the staff, the equipment and the financial resources to care for them the way we promised. The life's blood of the NHS is being leeched away by administrators thinking its function is to provide statistics, doctors thinking its function is to provide them with golf club dues, and private medicine paring away good staff and easy patients and leaving the Health Service to cope with what's left. It was a brilliant, humane conception, the envy of the world, and it's falling apart because of bureaucracy, laziness and greed.

'Then my father became ill. Progressive renal insufficiency. He was 58. Nobody gave a damn. No,' he corrected himself: he was thinking aloud, barely aware of my presence, 'that's not strictly fair. They cared, some of them, but the

152

economics of the business limited the help they could offer, on the National Health. He was going to die of a controllable condition because he was too old to be officially worth saving. My father is a musician, he teaches the violin. At 58 he had ten, fifteen, twenty more years of good work in him. Also, I love him.

'Only when I had tried every other avenue did I go to Barnes. I was desperate enough by then to swallow my principles. I knew his reputation – I knew I couldn't afford him. I thought probably he wouldn't do anything anyway. I had nothing to lose by asking, but God, I hated having to.

'Have you any idea what renal treatment costs? – whether you're talking of a transplant or a place on a dialysis programme. I told him what the position was, there seemed no point in lying. He was polite but distant: he said he'd give some thought to my problem and I thought that was the last I'd hear from him. But he called me the next day and said that if he could find a kidney that was a good match, that no younger patient had a better claim on, he'd do the transplant at a nominal cost as part of his research.

'You can imagine how I felt. I was over the moon, limp with relief. I didn't take much time to think what, beside the nominal expenses, I would end up paying for it. I think maybe I preferred not to give it too much thought. Dad was admitted to the Schaefer Clinic, all his tissue-type details were put on their computer and we waited. They were giving him dialysis now, so time wasn't as critical as it had been. All the same, it was getting on. It began to look as if finding a surgeon willing to do it was the easy part.

'Even in normal circumstances it's a kind of fiendish Chinese puzzle. Nobody knows when or where a kidney is going to became available. The best source is accident victims – people dying of head injuries. If they're dead on arrival there is very little time before the organ starts to deteriorate. You have to find the next of kin, get their consent, type the kidney, work out which of the would-be recipients has the best chance of accepting it, remove it, transport it – maybe the full length of the country – and install it, with the clock against you every step of the way.

'Another kind of clock was against my father. Because of his age, his priority was way down: the only chance, almost, was if a kidney turned up which was suitable for him and not for anyone else. Twice we were alerted to a possibility only to have the option taken up by someone with a better claim. In the end, when we couldn't get one any other way, I stole one.'

I doubt if there was much colour in my face by then, but what there was I felt draining away at that. My voice was a mere breathy croak. 'You did *what?*'

At my evident horror Ben managed a weary smile. Wonderful, isn't it, how just when you think that at least all the awfulness you've had to endure has rendered you shock-proof life finds some little way of showing you different.

'Come on, now, Clio,' he said, his kind sad eyes meeting mine for the first time since he began his confession, 'what I did was bad enough but it wasn't that bad. Of course I didn't kill anyone. The kidney came from a woman who'd finished with it and with everything else. It was a good match. No one else was asking for it. And the husband wouldn't consent.

'She was brain-dead, on a ventilator. A riding accident. She was only twenty-three. The hospital had alerted Julian as soon as she came in – there was never any hope for her. I raced up there and pleaded with the man to sign the release, but he wasn't interested. He cursed me for intruding on his grief. He wouldn't have her cut up, he said. The whole back of her head was caved in and he wouldn't agree to a neat surgical incision. I told him that when they pulled the plug on the ventilator it wouldn't make any difference to his wife or to him, but it would destroy a bit of tissue that would let my father live. He walked out on me.

'So I forged the papers. It wasn't difficult, I knew the

154

procedure and doctors have a quite touching way of trusting other doctors. I got the kidney, took it back to the clinic and later that day it was in my father. It still is. That was two years ago.'

I whispered incredulously, 'And they never found out?'

'Apparently not. I was sure they would. My heart was in my mouth the whole time. I couldn't believe it when they actually let me leave with the thing. Clio, I've never driven down a motorway so carefully in all my life. Then, after I got used to the idea that they weren't chasing me, I was sure they'd be waiting at the clinic; but they weren't, and after that I didn't much care. Once the thing was installed in my father no one was going to take it out, and if I had to face the consequences I would. I knew it would mean my career. I won't say I didn't care about that – I cared a lot. But it was my father's life, against a risk of discovery that grew less every day.

'I don't know how I got away with it: if I was just unbelievably lucky, or if someone covered up for me, or – I don't know. I was sweating for a month. But Dad was looking better than he had for years and I didn't regret what I'd done, not for a moment. I still don't. Not that part.

'You must understand, I was enormously grateful to Julian Barnes. With my father still seeing him it was inevitable that we should meet from time to time. I admired him. I even said that if there was ever anything I could do for him I'd jump at the chance. I meant it too, it wasn't just one of those things you say, after all there were elements of his work that I might be able to help with. I never *dreamt* –

'He never took me up on it, until a couple of weeks ago he telephoned me at home to say that a young friend of his was on his way round to me having taken his own life in rather embarrassing circumstances. Without actually saying so he made it quite clear that he expected me to carry out the most cursory of PMs and reach the most obvious of conclusions.

155

He didn't exactly say this either, but he also made it quite clear that he knew how I got my father's kidney. He made a kind of joke about it: he said he didn't know which would be worst, if the authorities got to hear of it or if my Father did.'

He looked up briefly, almost defiantly. 'I don't expect you to believe this, but I don't think I'd have done it. I had a lot to lose, and having come this far I was no longer resigned to losing it, and though I was shocked to the core by Barnes' threat I didn't doubt his readiness to carry it out. But I think I'd have let him rather than sign a report saying Luke Shaw committed suicide. I can't prove it, even to myself, but I think I would.

'Anyway, it didn't come to that. When you convinced Harry Marsh it was murder, of course he told me and then there was no way I could have palmed him off with a fudged PM, even if I'd wanted to. I called Barnes and told him so, and after a long and rather nasty pause he agreed it would probably do more harm than good. He –' For the first time in his extraordinary narrative he stopped.

I knew why. I said bleakly, 'He sent you to see me.'

We had walked – mechanically, step for robot step, without any awareness of where we were going or why – beyond the hospital compound and ended up in a bus shelter. We had it to ourselves. Those familiar with British public transport know well that bus shelters occupy some of the most desolate locations on earth, far from human habitation and remote from the traveller's way, undisturbed except on rare occasions even by the arrival of buses. There was no immediate likelihood of one happening along to interrupt us in our grim dialogue. It was a Tuesday.

'He did. I agreed. It seemed innocuous enough – '

'Innocuous?' I half-choked on the word, half-shouted it. I had held my peace thus far, partly from a kind of horrid fascination, partly because hearing him tell it I could not deny him some small sympathy, trapped as he had been between fate and Julian Barnes. But this was too much, too demeaning: he was putting what had happened to me on a par with – oh, I don't know, a bit of confidence trickery perhaps. 'And was it also innocuous when you passed on to him everything I told you, everything I found out and suspected, so that he knew when he had to silence me too?'

He sat on the bench, hunched and wretched, looking at his feet. But still he seemed unconscious of the enormity of what he had done. A shiver of pure primitive fear ran up my spine. What was Julian Barnes, that he could wreak such havoc on a human conscience? – that he could take men, layabouts like Harwich and Chandos but also a caring man like Ben Sawyer, sprinkle a little help over them and change them into monsters; or not even so much monsters as homunculi, artless passionless and unfeeling servants of his tyrant will? In earlier days he would have burned at the stake; or he would have conquered an empire.

I stood over him – just barely, with him seated and me standing I just had the advantage of height – and quite gently raised his chin so that his unwilling eyes met mine. 'Ben. I told my landlord I'd be leaving the flat because you asked me to. And then I found that cleared the way for an attempt on my life that was supposed to look like suicide. Innocuous? They were going to kill me with bloody bleach.'

He squirmed in my grip and my gaze. 'I didn't know. I swear I didn't know that. Julian told me what to say: he called me, when you left the clinic, he made me promise to call him back – ' After he had talked to me. After he had found out what I had done, what I was going to do. When they could be sure it was safer to kill me than to let me live. Hence the unlikely emergency in the morgue, that gave him time to call Barnes and get his new instructions. 'I didn't know what he intended.'

I shook my head. 'Between 1933 and 1945 Germany was almost entirely populated by people who didn't know things.

157

You didn't want to know. There was nothing else he could have intended. He had already killed two people: you knew that, whatever made you think he'd stop at me?'

I let go of him and turned my back, walking leadenly to the open door of the shelter. I leaned my head on my arm on the concrete upright and looked up the desolate road at nothing. 'Do you want a laugh? I thought it was Charlie. The longer it went on, the surer I was that someone was tipping Barnes off. I thought it was Charlie; even when we were on the run together. He made a phone call – to Harry Marsh, he said it was and it turned out he was telling the truth, but I thought – But it was me. Betraying us. I told you everything I knew, everything I suspected. I spoke to you after I'd seen Barnes and he set his dogs on me. I called you from the service station, and twenty minutes later they were in the car-park. And when it was all over I called you from the hospital, and one hot little phone call later Barnes was playing musical trains while the police were trying to surround his house without walking on the lawns.'

I wanted – I really wanted and needed – to be angry with him, to curse him and shrivel him and carve up his soul; but the anger would not come. I had chewed up Harry Marsh for something that was not his fault; now I was talking to Ben Sawyer in dull grey platitudes as if he was a kid I'd caught cheating in an exam and it didn't matter to me except that I regretted to see his career written off. It might have been that treacherous aftermath of shock; or that the squandered rage had finally run out; but I think really it was more to do with Ben. Shouting at him would have been like kicking a cripple.

I looked back at him and pushed a wan smile on to my face. 'You've got to admit, it's one for the record books – a whodunnit where Sherlock Holmes finally traces the crime to Doctor Watson.' He didn't think it was funny. Maybe it wasn't. I sighed. 'I should have seen it before now. Charlie wanted to know what was so special about Skipley, that people should go out of their way to kill and be killed here. You were the reason. In Skipley, dead bodies end up on your slab, and Barnes had every reason to suppose he could count on your co-operation. Without a tame pathologist he couldn't have taken the risk. You'd have done what he asked, Ben. He knew, and I know. Barnes murdered Luke, and the boy, and Harwich and Chandos helped him, but you were the one who made it possible. You are the one responsible.'

He looked at me with anguish in his eyes. 'I never touched Luke. I never wanted to hurt you. I made a couple of phone calls, that's all.'

'They were the wrong phone calls. You could have told the police. You could have told me. Okay, you acquired a kidney unlawfully. You did it to save the life of someone you loved. Maybe the GMC would have thrown the book at you, but most ordinary decent people would have understood. It was a hell of a jump from there to conniving at four murders. It's no thanks to you that Charlie and me didn't go the same way as Luke and the boy. Barnes' hoodlums did. You could have stopped it at any time. You're as guilty as sin.'

His head bowed. His long body was bent and awkward, like something broken; his voice was a whisper. 'How did you know?'

It was the most trivial thing he could have asked. I felt my lip curl and the taste of contempt like vomit in my throat. 'My arm. It got hurt when the Barnes Mafia came to my room. They knew but no one else did, not even Charlie. If you knew you had to have talked to them, or someone who was in touch with them, in the time between my arm getting hurt and them getting dead. You knew. They told Barnes when they called to say they'd lost us, Barnes told you when you told him where we were. When you hugged me, you shouldn't have been so careful.'

He was nodding, ponderously, his bent body rocking on the bench like a gentle idiot's. A trance-like glaze had crept

159

across his eyes. Unable to cope with the inexorable collapse of his life in fragments about him, despite the desperate measures he had taken to shore it up, he was retreating deep into his safe and secret mind; and it occurred to me, watching him gently rocking, that it could be a little while before he would be fit to stand trial.

Or he may have been taking a rest from reality rather than losing his grip on it, because he still knew what was important. 'What will you do now – tell the police?'

I leaned back against the concrete wall. 'No, you will.' He didn't understand. His expression remained vacant. I explained it simply, in words of few syllables. 'You tell them, Ben. Tell them what you want. Tell them about the kidney or don't, that's nothing to do with me. Tell them you wouldn't have faked the PM report, and that you didn't know why Barnes wanted reports on my activities. Tell them what you like, whatever you think they'll believe. But if you tell them nothing else, tell them where he is.'

'Barnes? I don't know where he is.'

I felt a band of muscle tightening around my chest. 'Ben, I swear to God, if you cover for him now – '

'Truly, Clio, I don't know. After you called me, last night, I called him. I told him you were safe, you were with the police and they were coming for him. I told him it was all over, and he rang off. That's all I know.' It was the truth. He hadn't the guts to lie.

I left him sitting alone in the shelter, a desolate frail figure, all the sap gone from him, and I walked quickly back to the hospital, sniffing angrily because I finally wanted to cry and I hadn't got a handkerchief.

FOUR

The idea came to me in the early evening and was so bizarre
that it quickly grew to conviction. Harry Marsh was not in
his office and he was not at the hospital. Charlie wrote his
home number on his magic slate and one of the nurses read it
over the phone to me.

Harry greeted me cautiously. I wasted no time on polite
conversational preamble. 'You keep telling me how easy this
has all been for me, because of my intimate knowledge of
those concerned. You also keep saying how I should not flit
round testing theories on my own but should pass my suspicions on to someone qualified to deal with them, i.e. you. All
right, this is your big chance. I'm going to share with you the
triumph and the glory if I'm right, the certainty of looking a
complete bloody idiot if I'm wrong. Interested?'

'Of course,' he said tersely. I had left him little option. I
had not intended to.

'I think I know where Barnes is, or at least how to find him.
I have no proof; I have no evidence. Only inspiration, based
on that intimate knowledge you're so envious of. Still
interested?'

'Fascinated.'

'Pick me up. My car's in a couple of buckets in the yard
behind your nick.'

People are endlessly surprising. I expected him to turn up
in something substantial, expensive and very slightly flash –

161

one of the racier Volvos, perhaps, or a Lancia. Instead he escorted me out to a long low Riley, liveried in brown and cream, its blue diamond badge mounted proudly before the gleaming, back-swept grill. Chrome glinted along the shapely flanks towards the graceful boat-shaped stern, and split the raked windscreen in half. It was beautiful. It must have been thirty years old. I roared with laughter.

'That thing'll be about as much use in a chase as mine!'

Harry grinned, patting the fabric roof affectionately. 'Yes, but you get a better class of incision with the headlamps.'

Inside it was leather, wood and elbow-to-elbow intimacy: a tight semi-sporting cockpit that positively encouraged the arm-round-the-shoulder style of motoring but made it impossible to take a promising relationship any further. I wondered if Harry found that a disadvantage.

I wasn't about to find out. Harry was preoccupied, so much so that when I played hard to get over the nature of my bizarre theory he declined to press me. It was disappointing, rather, but I guessed why and when it became obvious that he was not going to broach the subject I did. 'Do I gather you've seen Ben Sawyer this afternoon?'

He shot me a calculating look out of the corner of his eye. There was a certain amount of relief in it but not a great deal of surprise. 'You know about that?'

'Why do you think he suddenly decided to come clean? Guilty conscience on a slow fuse?'

'You guessed?'

'I deduced,' I said, not without a certain smugness. 'Using my intimate knowledge of a man I've known for a fraction of the time you have.'

'Ah, but perhaps less intimately,' he said. We grinned at each other. Harry went on, more seriously, 'It explained things, of course; but I was sorry to hear it.'

'Me too.' Lord, how the time was passing. Where was the passion gone? 'Will they give him a hard time?'

He stared ahead, concentrating on the night-bright road framed in the narrow windscreen. At length he said, 'There was blackmail. They'll take that into account. But yes, they'll give him a hard enough time.'

When the Riley pulled off the motorway and descended into the garden suburbs where the Schaefer Clinic nestled comfortably among the desirable residences of stockbrokers and advertising executives, Harry said, 'If I'm not to look an entire idiot, shouldn't I know what we're doing here?'

It did not seem an unreasonable request. 'Well, it's like this. Suppose it became of vital importance to you to hide a tree.'

'A tree?'

'A tree. Where would you put it?'

Harry viewed me in suspicious snatches as and when the traffic allowed. He was clearly entertaining the idea that the strain had finally proved too much and I had flipped my lid. Then he seemed to consider the possibility that he had. At last he answered doubtfully, 'A wood?'

'Splendid,' said I heartily, 'I'll make a detective of you yet. Then where do you hide a doctor?'

'Oh come on,' he said disgustedly, 'you don't really think we took their word for it that he'd skipped the clinic? We turned the bloody place inside out. That's how the private eye myth got started,' he added in a dark mutter, 'Conan Doyle making his policemen as thick as short planks so his hero would look brilliant by comparison. I suppose your books are like that – bloody patronising.'

'Of course you looked,' I agreed, patronisingly, 'and of course he isn't there. Even Julian Barnes wouldn't have that much effrontery. But he hasn't been on a train since the station masters wore top hats and the porters called you Sir, and with the rest of his life at stake he's not interested in breaking new ground. We'll find him in the kind of environment he knows, even if we have to look for him in unexpected ways.' And that, deliberately enigmatic, was all I would say until we had parked outside the Schaefer Clinic and trotted up the rosy brick steps that led to the glass swing doors.

Ben Sawyer was right about one thing: private medicine is a whole different world to the National Health Service. The absence of pressure is something quite extraordinary to someone at home in an NHS hospital. So is the decor. The foyer at the Schaefer Clinic was tastefully non-committal in cool gold and leaf green, the corners rounded off its geometric designs for fear they might make some kind of statement. The glass was bronzed and the metalwork was gold anodized. The place was quiet: partly because of a dark-green carpet a flock of Cotswold lions had spent a whole year growing but mostly because there was no evening rush on. That same lack of pressure facilitates a certain liberality regarding visiting hours. When a scabby-kneed schoolboy who looked like any other except for his suntan but who was probably heir to half of Abu Dhabi had been escorted out by what may have been the last English nanny actually working in England, we had it to ourselves.

I remember hospital receptionists from the bad old days when I had to work for a living. Few gave the impression of having been chosen by the interior decorator. This one remembered me, from my previous visit, and the expensive smile wavered even before Harry introduced himself and showed her his ID. It vanished altogether when I told her what I wanted.

She said frostily, 'I have absolutely no authority to disclose clinic records to you.'

'Listen, love,' I said wearily, 'I have been given a hard time by experts; some of them not unknown to you. Mr Barnes is sought by the police in connection with murder charges, not by the Inland Revenue for tax evasion. Now, Chief Inspector Marsh can go away and come back with a search warrant, in a police car with the two-tone on

164

maximum volume. Or I can wait until a Rolls-Royce pulls up outside and then start explaining again to you what it is I want, and why, in a loud voice. Or you can very discreetly pass me your admissions, discharges and transfers and I will sit quietly in that corner over there and read them, and no one need ever know.'

She thought about it. She thought about calling for directions; then it crossed her mind, visibly, that with Barnes gone she did not know who to call. She laid two books and a card index on the counter between us. She said in her perfect teeth, 'I hope you haven't left a squad car on the forecourt.'

Harry shook his head. 'Ours is the Morris Minor.' Her nostrils flared as if he'd shown her something disgusting.

His expression carefully deadpan, he followed me to the bronze glass coffee-table I had indicated. He swept copies of county magazines, all of them current, on to a vacant chair and watched me lay out the records and go to work. 'What are you looking for, exactly?'

'A patient who left here but never came. Ostensibly in for plastic surgery, I would guess, so there'd be lots of nice heavy facial dressings. And rather than leaving here to go home, he'll have been sent on to another private clinic, inside the UK but outside the Birmingham area. Last night, at short notice.'

Harry regarded me with acute interest, a tiny frown between his brows. When he realised what I was saying he blinked and his jaw dropped. 'Good God.'

It took a little time because he had been cleverer than that. He had faked the admission too, only the entry was in a different hand to the others for the same period – the same hand that recorded the transfer. Mr Ranjit Patel, a Birmingham businessman, had apparently suffered burns to his face and throat during a fire at his warehouse. After receiving treatment at the Schaefer Clinic he had been transferred, curiously late in the previous evening, to a convalescent home in Edinburgh.

'The convalescent home is of course run by a friend of his, or maybe someone else who owed him a favour. When Ben told him the police were on their way here he gave someone a fiver to take his car round to the station. He called Edinburgh, he arranged for transport and he forged the records. Then he told everyone he was going home and retired to an empty room to swathe himself in bandages. Face so he won't be recognised, throat so he won't have to speak.

'When the transport arrives the driver asks for Mr Patel, the receptionist finds him in the book and they collect him from his room. And they whip him off to safety in Edinburgh, where nobody's looking for him, where nobody's likely to look. Even if they did they'd be looking for an English doctor, not an Asian patient. He could stay there for weeks, without anyone but his friend knowing that under the bandages was undamaged skin. If his nurse thought the rest of him was pale for an Asian she wouldn't dream of commenting on it.'

I found Harry staring at me with wide, slightly glazed eyes in which warred disbelief and a kind of reluctant admiration. 'The jammy bastard!' His gaze hardened. 'So how much of this do you know and how much are you just guessing?'

Pleased with his response, I assured him airily, 'It's all guesswork. The indisputable facts are solely and simply as you see them. Maybe the clinic records are a bit slapdash, maybe it's all coincidence, maybe the chap they whipped off to Edinburgh really was the unfortunate Mr Patel and Julian Barnes is even now haunting the pontoons of Brighton Marina. You're the detective – what do you think?'

He gave it some consideration. 'I think one of us is in the wrong job.'

I grinned. 'Edinburgh?'

'Edinburgh.'

It's a long haul up from Birmingham. We drove through the

166

night. Twice we stopped for a breather at transport cafés. Once Harry let me take the wheel for an hour while he got some sleep. I gathered this was a considerable honour and treated the Riley with every reverence, at least until my companion had slumped down into a snoring bundle of raincoat.

In the glorious days of her youth, which were also the distant days of mine, that Riley had been able to pursue, though never quite to catch, a hundred miles an hour. Those days were gone; still, at that time of night, with juggernauts outnumbering cars decisively by numbers and overwhelmingly by tonnage, there was an illusion of speed that helped to sustain the sensation of progress.

Through the dark hours there were no cities to mark our way, only an occasional orange glow against the sky and a flurry of signs to herald a sliproad. Otherwise there were only headlamps racing south, sprung up and passed by in a matter of seconds, and ahead the high wide tail-lights of the thundering giants taking our own road north. On the flat they were the match of us, but on the hills the eager Riley engine deepened a tone as her wheels bit into the gradiant; hauling out, for a moment she ate spray – there had been a light rain all the way up from Stoke – and then she was clear, growling lustily up their long dark flanks and swinging back into the sudden glare of their headlamps. On long hills we took two or three at a time, me and the Riley both enjoying an imaginary Le Mans that defied the attempts of the speedometer to bind us to a pedestrian 55 mph.

Once the illusion was shattered by a dark panther of a sports car, or it may have been a low-flying aircraft, wailing past at about twice our speed. Twenty miles up the road there were accident warning signs and I saw him again, in a thousand tiny high-gloss pieces and a few larger ones, scattered over 200 yards of motorway, mostly on the far side of the crash barrier. The police were already on the scene. I paused briefly to see if I could help.

The policeman grimaced. 'It's not a doctor he needs now, thank you, miss, it's harp lessons.' I drove on and Harry hadn't stirred. Later he drove again and I slept like the dead.

I woke to a bleary northern dawn on which the incipient spring had as yet made little impact. The trees were still brown and skeletal, and above the nacrous veil of the new light the pale sky was as hard as an icicle. The rain had stopped. There was frost in the gutters.

I thought the Riley's engine was making a funny noise but it was Harry, humming softly and tunelessly to himself as he steered with one hand and shaved with the other – which is not, in all conscience, the standard of driving you expect from a police officer of twenty-four years' standing.

I looked around. We were off the motorway, on to some dreary sub-arterial lined spasmodically by one-man garages, two-lorry haulage firms, old grim cottages, new brash road-houses, and separating them the scrubby leprous land of failed smallholdings. Through a mouth that tasted of old socks I growled, 'Where the hell are we?'

'Nearly there.'

I scowled at him. I didn't believe we were nearly any-where. I thought perhaps we'd died in the night and this was purgatory: a linear community yards wide and miles long, whose only focus was the road, whose only life was rooted in the casual trade which marked the wake, along with tyre rubber and rusted exhausts, of the ever-passing traffic. I doubted the place even had a name.

But gradually we came into an orderly world of city out-works – not suburbs exactly – and the landmarks began to appear: the high craggy mound of Arthur's Seat, the curious pot-pourri of structures on Calton Hill, the unmistakable thrusting eminence of Castle Rock, its outline a confusing amalgam of natural and man-made features lowering over the city that grew up under its protection. We found the rising ridge of the Royal Mile, at that early hour a deserted ghost of the mediaeval city, and crossed Princes Street into a New Town apparently populated exclusively by milkmen. We stopped once to ask directions. Then we went to get some breakfast.

FIVE

The Hopefield Convalescent Home was also a private establishment, but there all similarity to the Schaefer Clinic ended. Where the one appeared a hybrid of a poodle parlour and one of the trendier banks, the other was a direct-line descendent of the cottage hospitals that served our parents' Britain in the first half of this century. Most of them are closed now, mainly because doctors can't work up the same enthusiasm for the little every-day hospital that used to deal so competently with the more routine aspects of the national health as they can for the gleaming centralised technopolis where they do everything but head transplants and they're working on that. Now patients needing tuppenny-ha'penny tonsil ops are kept waiting until they're septic, and then accommodated twenty miles from home in beds that cost a small fortune daily because of the specialist care and equipment on hand. It's a pity there's a limit to the amount of expertise you can exercise over a tonsil. Oh, brave new world.

The Hopefield Home was maybe half of a Georgian terrace originally built as family houses. As substantial as the Schaefer Clinic was airy, its massive ashlar masonry bore the grime of nearly two centuries like a black cloak; except at one end, where a facelift had begun to reveal the original buttermilk buff. Instead of bronze plate-glass it had twelve-pane windows, dozens of them, all painstakingly outlined in white;

instead of a foyer like the VIP lounge of a new airport, the high strong brass-appointed door gave on to a vista of parquet flooring, leather chairs grouped in small discreet cliques on large rugs, surveyed by black marble busts and two rubber trees. It might have been a private club or a very good hotel.

It was a lengthy trek from the door to the reception desk. As we crossed the public area, quite deserted at eight o'clock in the morning, I said out of the corner of my mouth, 'Will you do the talking or shall I?'

Harry sniffed. 'It's a murder enquiry. I will.'

'On the other hand, if I'm wrong I only make a fool of my myself and leave. If I'm wrong and you make a fool of yourself, you could end up supervising Boys' Brigade parades and directing traffic on market day.'

'True,' he said. 'It's only a theory. You can.'

The receptionist appeared in response to the bell. She greeted us with a smile. 'You're up early.'

I smiled back. 'Actually, we're up late. We've just driven up from the Schaefer Clinic in Birmingham. I'm Dr Rees. It's about a patient trasnsferred here yesterday – Mr Patel?' So, without a word of a lie, I succeeded in giving an entirely fallacious impression – a small skill but mine own.

She checked the record. 'That's right, the burns case. Is there some problem?'

'I need to have a word with him, that's all.'

I could see her wondering if the telephone hadn't reached Birmingham yet. She said, only a little doubtfully, 'I'm sure that will be all right – with you coming so far, too. Perhaps you should just have a word with Matron first?' I would have preferred not, of course, but she was already on the phone. 'Matron will see you now.' We proceeded as directed.

Matron was a largish, squarish, immensely competent-looking woman whom I had mentally categorised as middle-aged before I realised with a small shock she was about the same age as me. She didn't even look older, just more suitably dressed in a tailored two-piece and sensible shoes. Her broad forehead shored up a well-judged quantity of slightly faded blonde curls, which would still have gone neatly into a starched cap if required, and her eyes were a bright and humorous grey, shrewd and intelligent and altogether attractive. She was so perfect she could have been made from a kit of matron parts. It was impossible to think of her as a conspirator.

But she was and I knew it, because when I stopped thinking of her as a model of sensible mature womanhood such as I was sure I ought to be conforming to and wasn't, I realised that I knew her.

'Cath! Cath – er – ' My brain squirmed after memory.

'Holland,' she supplied, beaming. She gave every indication of being delighted to see me. 'Clio Rees! – it is still Rees?'

'It is indeed,' I said feelingly. 'Good grief, Cath, this is a long way from the Royal.'

It was not history's most tactful remark, and as soon as it was out I remembered that although Cath Holland had begun training with me – and Barnes, and God knows how many others – she had dropped out half-way through, following a family crisis of some kind. I hadn't thought of her since. Now I was a lapsed doctor and she was the matron of a private nursing home. Perhaps she had no regrets. It was still a clumsy thing to have said.

She took it in good part. It still had not struck her, the significance of my improbable arrival. 'I was born about five miles from here. I had to leave the Royal to look after my mother: you won't remember. When she died it seemed too late to go back to being a medical student, so I went into nursing instead.' She shrugged cheerfully. 'You always wonder how things might have been different, but I like my life. How about yourself? Are you working in London?'

'I live in London. I'm not working in medicine any more –

172

I'm a writer.'

She looked genuinely thrilled. 'Clio, how exciting! What do you write about?'

I said, 'Murder.' It was no more than the truth, but something in the way I said it – something I had not intended, perhaps a note of bitterness, of irony; something anyway of significance in the circumstances – intruded on the illusion of safety and good fellowship, and she realised that coincidence does not stretch as far as Barnes turning up one day and me the next. Clearly he had not warned her about me; clearly too she was on her guard against some development. I don't know what he had told her but she was no fool, she knew there was nothing jokey or inconsequential about his arrival here under an assumed identity. He had won her sympathy and the promise of her support with his damned plausible tongue, and if she did not know to expect me she was anyway keyed up to expect something. She must have feared the worst – even if only momentarily, before thrusting the dreadful thought to the very back of her mind. In her large face, shocked immobile, I saw the fear become reality.

Only her eyes continued to react, parading her horror, her disbelief, her grief and despair. Without a word from her, only by watching her eyes, I knew why she had taken him in, risked the life she had made for herself to protect him. She loved him: once, maybe still. He had never cared for her, not even when we were young and together and in and out of one another's beds and affections like yo-yos; but when he needed her the cynical bastard had turned on the charm and poor frustrated middle-aged Cath had come through for him. And I couldn't see any possible way of nailing him without crucifying her too.

When she finally spoke there was a pleading in her voice, but not for herself. 'What's going on, Clio? What are you doing here? Who's this gentleman with you?'

173

For a second I had forgotten he was there. 'The gentleman is Chief Inspector Marsh of Skipley CID. He's investigating the murder of my friend Luke Shaw and another, and the attempted murder of myself and another. He wants to interview one of your patients who was transferred here from the Schaefer Clinic in Birmingham.'

Well, that didn't leave much room for misunderstanding. Cath's large soft face crumpled like a failed soufflé. One moment she was there, strong and capable, holding up if under difficulties, and the next she was gone and all that remained was a collapsed, shrunken ruin of herself bereft of substance, diminished. She sank down behind the desk and even her chair noticed how much reduced she was and offered no complaint. God, I felt so sorry for her.

'Where is he?' I asked gently. Gently? – in the circumstances all the niceties in the world were meaningless and only the bare facts counted. The bare fact was that I was destroying her. 'Where, Cath? Which room?'

At the door of the second-storey room I stopped Harry with a hand in the middle of his chest. 'Wait here. Only a minute. Please?'

He viewed me with open suspicion. 'Not planning some more impromptu surgery, are you?'

I grinned, a shade tightly. 'It's a good idea. But I'm waiting for a new headlamp from sterile supplies.'

We compromised: I went in alone but left the door ajar.

He wasn't in bed. There was no reason he should have been; after all, there was nothing wrong with him. Wrapped in a paisley dressing-gown – none of your NHS boiled towelling here – he was sitting at the window, looking out on the square, a breakfast tray on the table beside him. If he had been there long he must have seen us arrive, although he had never met Harry and probably wouldn't recognise me from directly above. Still, he must have wondered, in view of the early hour. He was probably sitting there all tense and irritable, telling himself that if he froze up every time some-one came to the door he'd end up a nervous wreck in a different kind of lock-up to the one he was trying so valiantly to avoid.

A wicked notion insinuated itself into my mind.

I hissed at the open door, sotto voce: 'Don't be ridiculous, this one's a Paki!'

At the window Julian Barnes started visibly, as if he'd bumped into a defibrillator. I could see the back of his bandaged head wondering wildly what to do. He thought he knew my voice – but he might have been wrong: a case almost of seeing Feds under the bed. If he turned round he would know. But if he turned round and it was me, I might recognise him. Except that the bandages provided a compre-hensive disguise – as well they might, he had never applied bandages more carefully in all his life. Mr Patel, who had nothing to hide, would have turned to meet the uncouth intrusion – deliberately uncouth, I hasten to add, anyone who fancies his chances as a racist should avoid going into medicine, he'd get his eyes opened too often. By keeping his back stubbornly turned, particularly in view of such provo-cation, Barnes must have considered he would be more likely to arouse suspicion than allay it. He turned round.

I let him discover me tip-toeing back through the door. Spotted, I threw him an embarrassed and apologetic smile. 'I'm sorry, Mr Patel, I seem to have been given the wrong information. I was looking for someone else.'

He inclined his head in a slight, polite gesture of dismissal. All that showed of his face were his eyes. From recollection, I thought there was nothing remotely Asiatic in their colour-ing, but I didn't dare check for fear of striking that unmistak-able spark of recognition.

Still hovering tantalisingly close to the door I went on, 'I mean, how crazy can you get? They knew we were looking for a white – er, English gentleman. We needn't have disturbed

175

you at all.'

Like a wound in the white crepe, his lips forced a smile.

Fulsomely, I returned it. 'It's good of you to be so under-standing. It was just with you having come up from Birming-ham. The man we're looking for disappeared from the clinic where you were. But he was a doctor, not a patient, and a – um – native. Er – ' I leaned forward suddenly, staring him intently in the face. You could have cut the atmosphere with a scalpel. 'Those bandages look a little tight to me, Mr Patel. Would you like me to fix them for you? I am a doctor, I'm sure I could make you more comfortable.'

Barnes shook his swathed head vigorously.

I raised my fingers to his face. 'It only needs adjusting across here. It won't take a minute.'

If he'd been in less of a cold sweat, the turmoil inside him showing in his eyes like a vortex, he would have known immediately that his disguise was rumbled – that no doctor, not even an irresponsible former one given to writing lurid novels and wrecking other doctors' careers, would make that kind of approach to somebody else's patient. But he was no longer altogether rational. He had lived on his wits for too long, and then on his nerves, and now – facing an implacable Nemesis with no means of defending himself – he was dis-covering that the prospect of imminent destruction does nothing at all for the thought processes.

He jerked back from my hands and lurched round, and stood in the window trembling visibly. I should have taken pity on him then but, God forgive me, all I felt was an ice-cold exultation.

'All right, keep your hair on. You want it tight, you have it tight – it's no skin off my nose, though it might be some off yours. I'll go and leave you in peace – it's bloody hours back to Birmingham.' I closed the door crisply.

And stood waiting, still in the room, for him to calm his racing pulse, tell himself that I was gone and it was over, and turn round. It took perhaps twenty seconds; it felt much longer, probably for both of us.

When he saw me, and saw from my open regard that I knew him and had done all along, and that the undignified charade of the last minutes had been for nothing, a look of defeat washed into his eyes that no one who had known him before would ever have believed. His trembling had ceased; the fear was past. Despair is a calm and quiet thing. There was even a kind of relief in it, that the time of fanged and frantic hope was gone. He exhaled the last of it and inhaled only sterile hospital-issue air. Then he sat down in his chair at the window, not quite steadily because with the last of his hope had gone much of that strength and vitality that even those who didn't like him had always admired, and began to strip the bandages from his head.

'That was cruel.'

'Yes,' I agreed. 'But you're in no position to complain.'

'Now what?' The white crepe was piling up on the carpet.

'You can't guess?'

'Police, I suppose.'

'You got it in one.'

He said, 'You'll be responsible for the deaths of thousands.'

The sheer effrontery of the man was enough to make me gasp. 'I – ? Jesus, listen to Schweitzer!'

'I'm serious. I'm within months – eighteen, twenty-four at most – of an effective artificial implantable kidney. Thanks, I have to say, to the intervention of your friend Luke. If I'm free, wherever I am in the world and whoever's name I do it in, I can finish the work. That means the survival of people who will otherwise die. In prison I can't. That means people dying unnecessarily. The choice is yours.'

He looked straight at me. His face was white and drawn, stippled by the bandages, but still commanding, the diamond eyes still sharp and bright, compelling even in

177

defeat. I was reminded powerfully of the Ninevah lion, arrow-pierced and dying in the British Museum, still dangerous while breath lurked in the broken body. He would yet capture me with the mesmeric force of his Titan personality, if he could.

Anger is an under-rated emotion. We equate it with late buses, soggy toast and unadvertised changes in television programmes. 'God, that makes me angry,' we grit, when the waitress brings cold milk with the coffee or the kids put a roller-skate through the greenhouse glass, but it doesn't. Real anger has nothing to do with such situations. It begins, like indigestion, as a warmth and tension behind the breast-bone, spreading slowly but inexorably through the torso and limbs until all the body is clenched in a killing passion. The eyes burn, and behind them the functions of the mind narrow down to the immediate. Nothing impinges that is not directly concerned with the rage and its resolution: no fear, no pain, no conception of responsibility or consequence. The world shifts into a gloriously simple pattern of black and white with no greys; stimulus and response, with no considerations. It is anger, not courage or duty, which makes heroes. Usually it is anger which makes murderers. If I had still had Mrs Jackson's shotgun it would have made a murderer of me – if we accept Harry Marsh's judgement that I was not one already – and I don't think the fact that Harry was outside the door would have made any difference.

Contrary to the beliefs of a generation of playwrights, however, anger is not an articulate emotion. I had to fight for words to substitute for the violence which would have come naturally. My voice came out husky. 'That isn't true. You could have it published. If the work's as good as you say, someone would finish it.'

With something of the old hauteur, he raised an eyebrow. 'Give it away? After all I've done to protect it? That's my future. I shan't be long in prison. When I come out I shan't be able to practise: that process will be the only buffer between me and a quite unacceptable poverty. That's when I'll finish it. Then it'll not only keep me, it'll buy me back into a world that wouldn't have me at any other price. They may wrinkle their noses at me, but they won't turn them up at a functioning AIK. They can't afford to. I intend to be the richest ex-convict struck-off doctor in the history of medicine. Give it away? Give it a rest.'

He regarded me quizzically, almost smiling. He thought he had me over a barrel: that at the very least he had robbed my victory over him of any pleasure. He had forgotten that I had given up minstering to the sick in order to concentrate on mayhem. Also, he didn't know that there was a policeman outside his door. It might have made a difference to him, but it didn't to me.

I said, 'Julian, you have ridden roughshod over people all the years I have known you. Your career has been raised on the faces of those you've used – people like Ben Sawyer, people like Cath Holland. I suppose actually killing people to get what you want is only a logical extension of that.

'You're not going to believe this, and fortunately it doesn't matter whether you do or not, but if it were only Luke I'd be in trouble. I might think – in view of the stakes, and the way it began which was more accidental than deliberate, and the fact that you tried to scare him off, and the fact that if I kept silent Luke's death would enable you to complete something important and so not be entirely pointless – that what happened to him was something comparable to the fate of the shipwrecked mariner who draws the short straw and gets eaten by the others. His death wouldn't hurt any less, but it would make a kind of brutal sense if I thought you really had weighed it against the preventable misery of people you had a mission to save. I don't know what I'd have decided, but the thinking would have cost me blood.

'Thank Christ, you've spared me that. You've left me no

choice, and therefore no doubts. You shouldn't have killed the boy, Julian. Of all your mistakes, that was the biggest. You could have got away with it, but for him. I'd have accepted Luke's suicide, eventually, but for that poor little sod who had no business being there; and just possibly, but for him, I could have taken a short walk now while you packed a hasty bag and hailed a taxi.

'In spite of what I felt for him, or conceivably because of it, I could just possibly have been persuaded that there was a certain nobility in Luke's death, in your motives. But you killed that boy for no better reason than to dress up the set. You thought he made the scenario you'd devised that bit more plausible, and therefore made you that bit safer. A bit of insurance – that was the price of his life. Not the salvation of thousands, not the medical advance of the age – just a bit of extra insurance; belt and braces. You killed a sixteen-year-old boy the way normal people carry a plastic mac – for the peace of mind.'

He didn't understand. It wasn't a deliberate obtuseness, he genuinely didn't take my point. 'He was nobody. I never knew his name; I doubt if he remembered it himself. If I'd left him where I found him he'd have been dead anyway – now or soon.'

I shook my head; too vehemently, the anger was threatening to break through. 'He needn't have died. Jesus, Julian, he met a *doctor* - it should have been the luckiest day of his tragic little life.'

Barnes said coolly, 'It was. I gave him what he wanted – what he wanted most, and plenty of it. He died very, very happy.'

'Right enough, it sure as hell beats bleach.'

His eyes flickered guiltily. I do believe he had forgotten that. 'I never intended – '

'Didn't you? Your gorillas did. You mustn't have made your intentions entirely clear.'

180

He drew a deep breath that stiffened him. The firm jaw came up. Even seated, he could still look down his nose at me. 'You're going to betray me.'

I shook my head again. 'Only the good guys get betrayed. People like you get what's coming to them. Only usually they don't get it until it's too late.'

I pulled open the door and Harry Marsh was waiting, very close, and his eyes went round the room as if searching for blood.

6

We handed him over to the local constabulary for safe keeping. Harry made some phone calls and filled in some forms, and I made a statement. Another one. I kept it brief and, using my growing familiarity with this form of literary endeavour, managed to avoid reference to Cath Holland. I couldn't see how they could tie the investigation up without questioning her, but if she could – or would – use the respite to think up some answers which would put her in the clear, I wasn't about to rock that boat.

The administration of a police station bears a striking resemblance to that of a hospital. The only thing that works up a head of steam is the coffee machine. Matters proceeded at a pace so dignified as to verge upon the stately; lunchtime came and went, so did a plate of limp lettuce sandwiches. Finally, at about half past two, Harry stuck a weary head round the door and said, 'They've decided against charging us.' I thought he was joking, but I wasn't entirely sure.

They had finished with me before they finished with him so I had been waiting for some time, alone except for the remains of the rabbit's lunch, with nothing to do but worry. I had been worrying about the AIK.

It wasn't that I was buying Julian's blackmail. It was more that four people had died for it, including Luke, others had nearly died for it – including me – and yet others had wrecked careers, reputations and lives over the head of it.

Bought at such a price, it seemed incredible that the damn thing could be locked up in a bank vault or wherever for ten or fifteen years until Barnes should come back from the next-to-dead to claim it. I didn't share his confidence that he would be in and out of Winson Green like a dose of salts. Even when he was free there was no guarantee the work would be finished. There might not be the money, or the confidence, to back it; there might be compulsory euthanasia at forty-five and so enough transplants to go round; or someone else might come up with an AIK, in time to make Julian's redundant but still too late for a lot of people who were going to die of their disease in the next several years. The device Luke had died for was needed now, and I would not accept that the pique and selfishness of his murderer could be allowed to stand between those people and their salvation.

I stood up slowly. 'Can I see Julian Barnes?'

I didn't expect they would let me, so the celerity with which I was shown into the interview room took the wind out of my sails and left my mental processes in disarray. I didn't know what I wanted to say. I don't have that problem often.

Julian looked up from the table. He looked pale and tired, but in a distinguished way, not haggard. He managed to give the impression of a senior surgeon exhausted after twelve hours in the operating theatre who is called upon to explain the presence of his car in the Unit Administrator's parking space. That godhead aura hung still about him, thin in places and a little tattered but still largely intact. Even the worldly-wise policemen were conscious of its effect. He'd have a wonderful day in court. The jury would convict, they would have no choice, but they'd be as impressed as hell while they did it.

He said, very politely, 'Yes?'

I drew myself up to my full five-foot-two. 'I want your papers, Julian. I'll find the best man available to continue your work. ComIntel will do the micro-electronics. We'll make a good job of it. It'll carry your name, and whatever money there is after the costs are paid I'll keep safe for you. I'll get a contract drawn up. Everything you've done, in every sense, will be wasted if that AIK disappears now. If it's all you say – and it had better be – it can't wait for you.'

'I told you that, while the choice was yours.'

I flared my nostrils at him. 'Now it's yours. Give me the papers.'

He smiled, coldly. That cold smile was probably the last thing Luke saw, I thought. 'My dear, I fear that success has turned your head.'

My insides were beginning to quake with rage and frustration. I wanted to cry; I was crying, damn it, the tears were in my eyes and thick in my throat, but my heart was a savage brew of anger. 'You unutterable bastard,' I choked, 'I'll get you. I'll get you where it hurts.'

'Clio.' Harry's fingers locked like an iron ring on my upper arm. 'That's enough. Come away now.'

I resisted his strong hand, standing my ground stubbornly. My eyes never left Barnes' face. I hoped they might burn an imprint there he would feel for the rest of his days. 'I mean it. He knows I mean it, and what's more I'll do it without breaking a single law, common, enacted or moral. You want to make medicine an industry? Okay. Industrial espionage is not a crime. When all this comes out – and it will; by God it will – I'll get all the help I can use.

'Other people are involved in your work, Julian – normal people, people who'll throw a fit when they hear what you've done. Your technician – the one who made the blunder? He'll be as sick as a dog, he'll do anything I ask to try and balance the account. Your assistants, your staff, whoever has your papers: they'd have defended your work with their lives in other circumstances. But now? I don't even think I'll have to go looking for them. I think they'll come looking for me.'

He stared at me, ashen. 'That would not be – ethical.'

I laughed, immoderately. I roared with laughter. I laughed until the waiting tears flooded down my cheeks and I thought something vital to my continued well-being would burst. I laughed hysterically until Harry led me away and helped me down the steps, and in the hidden car-park behind the building held me against his chest while the mirth turned to grief and the laughter to uncontrollable weeping. I was terribly tired.

We were in the car and the throaty Riley engine was straining for the gate and the open road, more like an eager animal than a machine, when a constable came scuttling round the corner of the police station with a piece of paper fluttering in his hand. 'Haud oan, chief!' They talk funny in Scotland. North of England, too; and the Midlands. Well, anywhere north of Watford, really.

Harry wound down the window and the long arm of the law stretched across the narrow cockpit. 'It's for you, miss. From the doctor.'

The writing was a classic medical scrawl, as if written on the back of a cow with a length of half-cooked spaghetti, but when we deciphered it the words on one side were a name and address and on the other an instruction to surrender the documents held by that person to me.

The drive down was easier and pleasanter than the drive up, and took much longer. We stopped for tea at Gretna, for supper in Lancaster, and that night at a motel off the motorway where a river coursing under the back windows left low sandy islets for the swans to roost on.

Over breakfast Harry said, 'What will you do with it?'

There was no need to be more explicit. The impromptu consent sat on the table between us, folded neatly, a little like a talisman and a little like a bomb.

'Christ, *I* don't know,' I said irritably. 'Use it, I suppose. I think I have to. Luke's firm will help with the technical side, I'm sure of that. I'll have to find a medical scientist, preferably one already working on the renal system, who doesn't mind throwing up his own work in order to finish someone else's. They'll be queuing up in the street, won't they? Maybe the trust will help – the one that came up with the finance. Somebody has to. It can't end here.'

'Do you have to start today?'

I realised I was preaching at him and grinned. 'No, conditions of service in the world-saving business specify long weekends.'

'My mother wants you to spend a few days in the West Country.'

My mind, and I suspect also my face, did a couple of double-takes, a half-pass and a stall-turn. He might have been offering me a controlling interest in a stoat farm. Comprehension eluded me with contemptuous ease. 'Your mother – ?'

'My mother, Charlie's mother – remember? She wants to thank you in person. She hopes you'll pay her a visit.'

I was amazed, staggered to my bootheels. Of course, he could have got it wrong. 'Are you sure that's what she said? Maybe she wants to have a go at me with her walking stick.'

'My mother,' Harry said with some dignity, 'does not use a walking stick. She hunts twice a week in winter, goes on long-distance rambles in summer, and dances the legs off people half her age at every county ball. Anyway, she doesn't blame you for what happened to Charlie.' He sniffed. 'She blames me for what happened to Charlie.'

I shook my head, bemused. 'I don't know what to say.'

'There's no problem, is there?'

'No – ' I began doubtfully. Then I said it again, with conviction. 'No. I'd love to go.'

'That's good,' said Harry, 'because I told her you would.

You can drive Charlie home when they discharge him.'

'What *in*? My car's a banana split,' I reminded him frostily.

'Charlie's motor. He left it at my place, to avoid arousing suspicion. If you can drive the Riley you can manage a Porsche. It's only six months old,' he added with fine disdain.

I was getting very strange feelings about all of this. 'Porsche? Hunting? What the hell kind of a family are you?'

'A good one,' Harry said lugubriously. 'Charlie's side, that is. Mine's as common as muck. When my dad buggered off my mum looked on it as a heaven sent opportunity to better herself. Charlie's an Honourable. No wonder the poor sod feels he has to vote Liberal.'

I think I was more floored by that disclosure than by almost anything that had gone before. Harry finished his kipper and started into the toast while I struggled for composure. 'Charlie? Rich? Have you seen his *jeans*?' I ladled sugar absently into my coffee, and stirred it too, before remembering that I don't take it. I pushed the cup away, defeated. 'What about your mum? What's she like?'

'Daft as a brush,' Harry said briskly, 'you'll get on famously.'

I finally thought of something to say. I laced it with accusation. 'Why didn't you tell me any of this last night?'

Harry smiled, a warmth in his grey eyes. 'Preoccupied.'

Somewhere south of Warrington, the Riley trundling along in the middle lane with a song like a happy Spitfire, Harry observed thoughtfully, 'If you're going to be organising a new team at the Schaefer Clinic, I suppose you're likely to be in Birmingham quite a bit.'

I gave it some consideration. 'I imagine so. At least until the project's running smoothly again. I hope I haven't bitten off more than I can chew.' I had. I knew I had. Christ almighty, didn't I always?

Well on the way to Stoke he broached the subject again. 'If you intend to protect Barnes' interests, surely you'll have to stay involved – at least in an administrative capacity?

I gave that some thought too. 'I suppose I will. God rot the man, but I did promise.'

We were through Cannock before he made his final assault on the matter. His gaze fixed firmly ahead, his profile host to a fey little half-smile, he said, 'Still, if you're going to be organising important medical research, I expect you'll be kept pretty busy.'

'I expect so.'

'Too busy, for instance, for – '

I turned my head, owl-like, through ninety degrees – those Riley seats, which must have made a significant contribution to family planning in their day, discouraging any more bodily movement – and stared Harry Marsh sternly in his left eye. 'Too busy, for instance, for what?'

He met my gaze, eyebrows raised, his face innocent. 'For writing. Too busy for writing, I was going to say. I don't suppose there'll be any more books for a while.'

I glared at him with deep suspicion but he drove on blithely, regardless. Unable to crack him by psychological pressure I gave a quick snort of laughter and returned my eyes to the busy, bifurcating road. 'There'll be one more,' I said as we swung into Spaghetti Junction.